Thomas H. Huxley

Animal automatism and other essays

Thomas H. Huxley

Animal automatism and other essays

ISBN/EAN: 9783742833341

Manufactured in Europe, USA, Canada, Australia, Japa

Cover: Foto ©Andreas Hilbeck / pixelio.de

Manufactured and distributed by brebook publishing software
(www.brebook.com)

Thomas H. Huxley

Animal automatism and other essays

AND

OTHER ESSAYS,

VIZ.: SCIENCE AND CULTURE; ELEMENTARY INSTRUCTION IN PHYSIOLOGY; THE BORDER TERRITORY BETWEEN ANIMALS AND PLANTS; UNIVERSITIES, ACTUAL AND IDEAL.

BY THOMAS HENRY HUXLEY, LL.D., F.R.S.

I.

ON THE HYPOTHESIS THAT ANIMALS ARE AUTOMATA, AND ITS HISTORY.*

THE first half of the seventeenth century is one of the great epochs of biological science. For though suggestions and indications of the conceptions which took definite shape, at that time, are to be met with in works of earlier date, they are little more than the shadows which coming truth casts forward; men's knowledge was neither extensive enough, nor exact enough, to show them the solid body of fact which threw these shadows.

But, in the seventeenth century, the idea that the physical processes of life are capable of being explained in the same way as other physical phenomena, and, therefore, that the living body is a mechanism, was proved to be true for certain classes of vital actions; and, having thus taken firm root in irrefragable fact, this conception has not only successfully repelled every assault which has been made upon it, but has steadily grown in force and extent of application, until it is now the expressed or implied fundamental proposition of the whole doctrine of scientific Physiology.

If we ask to whom mankind are indebted for this great service, the general voice will name William Harvey. For, by his discovery of the circulation of the blood in the higher animals, by his explanation of the nature of the mechanism by which that circulation is effected, and by his no less remarkable, though less known, investigations of the process of development, Harvey solidly laid the foundations of all those physical explanations of the functions of sustentation and reproduction which modern physiologists have achieved.

But the living body is not only sustained and reproduced: it adjusts itself to external and internal changes; it moves and feels. The attempt to reduce the endless complexities of animal motion and feeling to law and order is, at least, as important a part of the task of the physiologist as the elucidation of what are sometimes called the vegetative processes. Harvey did not make this attempt himself; but the influence of his work upon the man who did make it is patent and unquestionable. This man was René Descartes, who, though by many years Harvey's junior, died before him; and yet, in his short

* An Address delivered at the meeting of the British Association for the Advancement of Science at Belfast, 1874.

span of fifty-four years, took an undisputed place, not only among the chiefs of philosophy, but amongst the greatest and most original of mathematicians; while, in my belief, he is no less certainly entitled to the rank of a great and original physiologist; inasmuch as he did for the physiology of motion and sensation that which Harvey had done for the circulation of the blood, and opened up that road to the mechanical theory of these processes, which has been followed by all his successors.

Descartes was no mere speculator, as some would have us believe: but a man who knew of his own knowledge what was to be known of the facts of anatomy and physiology in his day. He was an unwearied dissector and observer; and it is said, that, on a visitor once asking to see his library, Descartes led him into a room set aside for dissections, and full of specimens under examination. "There," said he, "is my library."

I anticipate a smile of incredulity when I thus champion Descartes's claim to be considered a physiologist of the first rank. I expect to be told that I have read into his works what I find there, and to be asked, Why is it that we are left to discover Descartes's deserts at this time of day, more than two centuries after his death? How is it that Descartes is utterly ignored in some of the latest works which treat expressly of the subject in which he is said to have been so great?

It is much easier to ask such questions than to answer them, especially if one desires to be on good terms with one's contemporaries; but, if I must give an answer, it is this: The growth of physical science is now so prodigiously rapid, that those who are actively engaged in keeping up with the present, have much ado to find time to look at the past, and even grow into the habit of neglecting it. But, natural as this result may be, it is none the less detrimental. The intellect loses, for there is assuredly no more effectual method of clearing up one's own mind on any subject than by talking it over, so to speak, with men of real power and grasp, who have considered it from a totally different point of view. The parallax of time helps us to the true position of a conception, as the parallax of space helps us to that of a star. And the moral nature loses no less. It is well to turn aside from the fretful stir of the present and to dwell with gratitude and respect upon the services of those "mighty men of old who have gone down to the grave with their weapons of war," but who, while they yet lived, won splendid victories over ignorance. It is well, again, to reflect that the fame of Descartes filled all Europe, and his authority overshadowed it for a century; while now, most of those who know his name think of him, either as a person who had some preposterous notions about vortices and was deservedly annihilated by the great Sir Isaac Newton; or as the apostle of an essentially vicious method of deductive speculation; and that, nevertheless, neither the chatter of shifting opinion, nor the silence of personal oblivion, has in the slightest degree affected the growth of the great ideas of which he was the instrument and the mouthpiece.

It is a matter of fact that the greatest physiologist of the eighteenth century, Haller, in treating of the functions of nerve, does little more than reproduce and enlarge upon the ideas of Descartes. It is a matter of fact that David Hartley, in his remarkable work the "Essay on Man," expressly, though still insufficiently, acknowledges the resemblance of his fundamental conceptions to those of Descartes; and I shall now endeavor to show that a series of propositions, which constitute the foundation and essence of the modern physiology of the nervous system, are fully expressed and illustrated in the works of Descartes.

I. *The brain is the organ of sensation, thought, and emotion; that is to say, some change in the condition of the matter of this organ is the invariable antecedent of the state of consciousness to which each of these terms is applied.*

In the "Principes de la Philosophie" (§ 169), Descartes says:—*

"Although the soul is united to the whole body, its principal functions are, nevertheless, performed in the brain; it is here that it not only understands and imagines, but also feels; and this is effected by the intermediation of the nerves, which extend in the form of delicate threads from the brain to all parts of the body, to which they are attached in such a manner, that we can hardly touch any part of the body without setting the extremity of some nerve in motion. This motion passes along the nerve to that part of the brain which is the common sensorium, as I have sufficiently explained in my Treatise on Dioptrics: and the movements which thus

* I quote, here and always, Cousin's edition of the works of Descartes, as most convenient for reference. It is entitled "Œuvres complètes de Descartes," publiées par Victor Cousin. 1824.

travel along the nerves, as far as that part of the brain with which the soul is closely joined and united, cause it, by reason of their diverse characters, to have different thoughts. And it is these different thoughts of the soul, which arise immediately from the movements that are excited by the nerves in the brain, which we properly term our feelings, or the perceptions of our senses."

Elsewhere,* Descartes, in arguing that the seat of the passions is not (as many suppose) the heart, but the brain, uses the following remarkable language:—

"The opinion of those who think that the soul receives its passions in the heart, is of no weight, for it is based upon the fact that the passions cause a change to be felt in that organ; and it is easy to see that this change is felt, as if it were in the heart, only by the intermediation of a little nerve which descends from the brain to it; just as pain is felt, as if it were in the foot, by the intermediation of the nerves of the foot; and the stars are perceived, as if they were in the heavens, by the intermediation of their light and of the optic nerves. So that it is no more necessary for the soul to exert its functions immediately in the heart, to feel its passions there, than it is necessary that it should be in the heavens to see the stars there."

This definite allocation of all the phenomena of consciousness to the brain as their organ, was a step the value of which it is difficult for us to appraise, so completely has Descartes's view incorporated itself with every-day thought and common language. A lunatic is said to be "crack-brained" or "touched in the head," a confused thinker is "muddle-headed," while a clever man is said to have "plenty of brains;" but it must be remembered that at the end of the last century a considerable, though much over-estimated, anatomist, Bichat, so far from having reached the level of Descartes, could gravely argue that the apparatuses of organic life are the sole seat of the passions, which in no way affect the brain, except so far as it is the agent by which the influence of the passions is transmitted to the muscles.†

Modern physiology, aided by pathology, easily demonstrates that the brain is the seat of all forms of consciousness, and fully bears out Descartes's explanation of the reference of those sensations in the viscera which accompany intense emotion, to these organs. It proves, directly, that those states of consciousness which we call sensations are the immediate consequent of a change in the brain excited by the sensory nerves; and, on the well-known effects of injuries, of stimulants, and of narcotics, it bases the conclusion that thought and emotion are, in like manner, the consequents of physical antecedents.

* "Les Passions de l'Ame," Article xxxiii.

† "Recherches physiologiques sur la Vie et la Mort." Par Xav. Bichat, Art. Sixième.

II. *The movements of animals are due to the change of form of muscles, which shorten and become thicker; and this change of form in a muscle arises from a motion of the substance contained within the nerves which go to the muscle.*

In the "Passions de l'Ame," Art. vii., Descartes writes:—

"Moreover, we know that all the movements of the limbs depend on the muscles, and that these muscles are opposed to one another in such a manner, that when one of them shortens, it draws along the part of the body to which it is attached, and so gives rise to a simultaneous elongation of the muscle which is opposed to it. Then, if it happens, afterward, that the latter shortens, it causes the former to elongate, and draws toward itself the part to which it is attached. Lastly, we know that all these movements of the muscles, as all the senses, depend on the nerves, which are like little threads or tubes, which all come from the brain, and, like it, contain a certain very subtle air or wind, termed the animal spirits."

The property of muscle mentioned by Descartes now goes by the general name of contractility, but his definition of it remains untouched. The long-continued controversy whether contractile substance, speaking generally, has an inherent power of contraction, or whether it contracts only in virtue of an influence exerted by nerve, is now settled in Haller's favor, but Descartes's statement of the dependence of muscular contraction on nerve holds good for the higher forms of muscle, under normal circumstances; so that, although the structure of the various modifications of contractile matter has been worked out with astonishing minuteness—although the delicate physical and chemical changes which accompany muscular contraction have been determined to an extent of which Descartes could not have dreamed and have quite upset his hypothesis that the cause of the shortening and thickening of the muscle is the flow of animal spirits into it from the nerves—the important and fundamental part of his statement remains perfectly true.

The like may be affirmed of what he says about nerve. We know now that nerves are not exactly tubes, and that "animal spirits" are myths; but the exquisitely refined methods of investigation of Dubois-Reymond and of Helmholz have no less clearly proved that the antecedent of ordinary muscular contraction is a motion of the molecules of the nerve going to the muscle; and that this motion is propagated with a measurable, and by no means great, velocity, through the substance of the nerve toward the muscle.

With the progress of research, the term "animal spirits" gave way to "nervous fluid," and "nervous fluid" has now given way to "molecular motion of nerve-substance." Our conceptions of what takes place in nerve have altered in the same way as our conceptions of what takes place in a conducting wire have altered, since electricity was shown to be not a fluid, but a mode of molecular motion. The change is of vast importance, but it does not affect Descartes's fundamental idea, that a change in the substance of a motor nerve propagated toward a muscle is the ordinary cause of muscular contraction.

III. *The sensations of animals are due to a motion of the substance of the nerves which connect the sensory organs with the brain.*

In *La Dioptrique* (Discours Quatrième), Descartes explains, more fully than in the passage cited above, his hypothesis of the mode of action of sensory nerves:—

"It is the little threads of which the inner substance of the nerves is composed which subserve sensation. You must conceive that these little threads, being inclosed in tubes, which are always distended and kept open by the animal spirits which they contain, neither press upon nor interfere with one another, and are extended from the brain to the extremities of all the members which are sensitive—in such a manner that the slightest touch which excites the part of one of the members to which a thread is attached, gives rise to a motion of the part of the brain whence it arises, just as by pulling one of the ends of a stretched cord, the other end is instantaneously moved. . . . And we must take care not to imagine that, in order to feel, the soul needs to behold certain images sent by the objects of sense to the brain, as our philosophers commonly suppose; or, at least, we must conceive these images to be something quite different from what they suppose them to be. For as all they suppose is that these images ought to resemble the objects which they represent, it is impossible for them to show how they can be formed by the objects received by the organs of the external senses and transmitted to the brain. And they have had no reason for supposing the existence of these images except this; seeing that the mind is readily excited by a picture to conceive the object which is depicted, they have thought that it must be excited in the same way to conceive those objects which affect our senses by little pictures of them formed in the head; instead of which we ought to recollect that there are many things besides images which may excite the mind, as, for example, signs and words, which have not the least resemblance to the objects which they signify."*

Modern physiology amends Descartes's conception of the mode of action of sensory nerves in detail, by showing that their structure is the same as that of motor nerves; and that the changes which take place in them, when the sensory organs with which they are connected are excited, are of just the same nature as those which occur in motor nerves, when the muscles to which they are distributed are made to contract: there is a molecular change which, in the case of the sensory nerve, is propagated toward the brain. But the great fact insisted upon by Descartes, that no likeness of external things is, or can be, transmitted to the mind by the sensory organs; but that, between the external cause of a sensation and the sensation, there is interposed a mode of motion of nervous matter, of which the state of consciousness is no likeness, but a mere symbol, is of the profoundest importance. It is the physiological foundation of the doctrine of the relativity of knowledge, and a more or less complete idealism is a necessary consequence of it.

For of two alternatives one must be true. Either consciousness is the function of a something distinct from the brain, which we call the soul, and a sensation is the mode in which this soul is affected by the motion of a part of the brain; or there is no soul, and a sensation is something generated by the mode of motion of a part of the brain. In the former case, the phenomena of the senses are purely spiritual affections; in the latter, they are something manufactured by the mechanism of the body, and as unlike the causes which set that mechanism in motion, as the sound of a repeater is unlike the pushing of the spring which gives rise to it.

* Locke ("Human Understanding," Book II., chap. viii. 37) uses Descartes's illustration for the same purpose and warns us that "most of the ideas of sensation are no more the likeness of something existing without us than the names that stand for them are the likeness of our ideas, which yet, upon hearing, they are apt to excite in us," a declaration which paved the way for Berkeley.

The nervous system stands between consciousness and the assumed external world, as an interpreter who can talk with his fingers stands between a hidden speaker and a man who is stone deaf—and Realism is equivalent to a belief on the part of the deaf man, that the speaker must also be talking with his fingers. "Les extrêmes se touchent;" the shibboleth of materialists that "thought is a secretion of the brain," is the Fichtean doctrine that "the phenomenal universe is the creation of the Ego," expressed in other language.

IV. *The motion of the matter of a sensory nerve may be transmitted through the brain to motor nerves, and thereby give rise to contraction of the muscles to which these motor nerves are distributed; and this reflection of motion from a sensory into a motor nerve may take place without volition, or even contrary to it.*

In stating these important truths, Descartes defined that which we now term "reflex action." Indeed he almost uses the term itself, as he talks of the "animal spirits" as "réfléchis,"* from the sensory into the motor nerves. And that this use of the word "reflected" was no mere accident, but that the importance and appropriateness of the idea it suggests was fully understood by Descartes's contemporaries, is apparent from a passage in Willis's well-known essay, "De Animâ Brutorum," published in 1672, in which, in giving an account of Descartes's views, he speaks of the animal spirits being diverted into motor channels, "velut undulatione reflexâ."†

Nothing can be clearer in statement, or in illustration, than the view of reflex action which Descartes gives in the "Passions de l'Ame," Art. xiii.

After recapitulating the manner in which sensory impressions transmitted by the sensory nerves to the brain give rise to sensation, he proceeds:—

"And in addition to the different feelings excited in the soul by these different motions of the brain, the animal spirits, without the intervention of the soul, may take their course toward certain muscles, rather than toward others, and thus move the limbs, as I shall prove by an example. If some one moves his hand rapidly toward our eyes, as if he were going to strike us, although we know that he is a friend, that he does it only in jest, and that he will be very careful to do us no harm, nevertheless it will be hard to keep from winking. And this shows, that it is not by the agency of the soul that the eyes shut, since this action is contrary to that volition which is the only, or at least the chief, function of the soul; but it is because the mechanism of our body is so disposed, that the motion of the hand toward our eyes excites another movement in our brain, and this sends the animal spirits into those muscles which cause the eyelids to close."

Since Descartes's time, experiment has eminently enlarged our knowledge of the details of reflex action. The discovery of Bell has enabled us to follow the tracks of the sensory and motor impulses, along distinct bundles of nerve fibers; and the spinal cord, apart from the brain, has been proved to be a great center of reflex action; but the fundamental conception remains as Descartes left it, and it is one of the pillars of nerve physiology at the present day.

V. *The motion of any given portion of the matter of the brain excited by the motion of a sensory nerve, leaves behind a readiness to be moved in the same way, in that part. Anything which resuscitates the motion gives rise to the appropriate feeling. This is the physical mechanism of memory.*

Descartes imagined that the pineal body (a curious appendage to the upper side of the brain, the function of which, if it have any, is wholly unknown) was the instrument through which the soul received impressions from, and communicated them to, the brain. And he thus endeavors to explain what happens when one tries to recollect something:—

"Thus when the soul wills to remember anything, this volition, causing the [pineal] gland to incline itself in different directions, drives the [animal] spirits toward different regions of the brain, until they reach that part in which are the traces, which the object which it desires to remember has left. These traces are produced thus: those pores of the brain through which the [animal] spirits have previously been driven, by reason of the presence of the object, have thereby acquired a tendency to be opened by the animal spirits which return toward them, more easily than other pores, so that the animal spirits, im-

* "Passions de l'Ame," Art. xxxvi.

† "Quamcumque bruti actionem, velut automati mechanici motum artificialem, in eo consistere quod se primò sensibile aliquod spiritus animales afficiens, eosque introrsum convertens, *sensionem* excitat, à qua mox iidem spiritus, velut undulatione reflexâ denuo retrorsum commoti atque pro concinno ipsius fabricæ organorum, et partium ordine, in certos nervos musculosque determinati, respectivos *membrorum motus* perficiunt,"—WILLIS: "De Animâ Brutorum," p. 5, ed. 1763.

pinging on these pores, enter them more readily than others. By this means they excite a particular movement in the pineal gland, which represents the object to the soul, and causes it to know what it is which it desired to recollect."*

That memory is dependent upon some condition of the brain is a fact established by many considerations—among the most important of which are the remarkable phenomena of aphasia. And that the condition of the brain on which memory depends, is largely determined by the repeated occurrence of that condition of its molecules, which gives rise to the idea of the thing remembered, is no less certain. Every boy who learns his lesson by repeating it exemplifies the fact. Descartes, as we have seen, supposes that the pores of a given part of the brain are stretched by the animal spirits, on the occurrence of a sensation, and that the part of the brain thus stretched, being imperfectly elastic, does not return to exactly its previous condition, but remains more distensible than it was before. Hartley suppose that the vibrations, excited by a sensory, or other, impression, do not die away, but are represented by smaller vibrations or "vibratiuncules," the permanency and intensity of which are in relation with the frequency of repetition of the primary vibrations. Haller has substantially the same idea, but contents himself with the general term "mutationes," to express the cerebral change which is the cause of a state of consciousness. These "mutationes" persist for a long time after the cause which gives rise to them has ceased to operate, and are arranged in the brain according to the order of co-existence and succession of their causes. And he gives these persistent "mutationes" the picturesque name of *vestigia rerum*, "quæ non in mente sed in ipso corpore et in medulla quidem cerebri ineffabili modo incredibiliter minutis notis et copia infinita, inscriptæ sunt."† I do not know that any modern theory of the physical conditions of memory differs essentially from these, which are all children—*mutatis mutandis*—of the Cartesian doctrine. Physiology is, at present, incompetent to say anything positively about the matter, or to go farther than the expression of the high probability, that every molecular change which gives rise to a state of consciousness, leaves a more or less persistent structural modification, through which the same molecular change may be regenerated by other agencies than the cause which first produced it.

* "Les Passions de l'Ame," xlii.

† Haller, "Primæ Lineæ," ed. iii. "Sensus Interni," dlviii.

Thus far, the propositions respecting the physiology of the nervous system which are stated by Descartes have simply been more clearly defined, more fully illustrated, and, for the most part, demonstrated, by modern physiological research. But there remains a doctrine to which Descartes attached great weight, so that full acceptance of it became a sort of note of a thorough-going Cartesian, but which, nevertheless, is so opposed to ordinary prepossessions that it attained more general notoriety, and gave rise to more discussion, than almost any other Cartesian hypothesis. It is the doctrine, that brute animals are mere machines or automata, devoid not only of reason, but of any kind of consciousness, which is stated briefly in the "Discours de la Méthode," and more fully in the "Réponses aux Quatrièmes Objections," and in the correspondence with Henry More.*

The process of reasoning by which Descartes arrived at this startling conclusion is well shown in the following passage of the "Réponses:"—

"But as regards the souls of beasts, although this is not the place for considering them, and though, without a general exposition of physics, I can say no more on this subject than I have already said in the fifth part of my Treatise on Method; yet, I will further state, here, that it appears to me to be a very remarkable circumstance that no movement can take place, either in the bodies of beasts, or even in our own, if these bodies have not in themselves all the organs and instruments by means of which the very same movements would be accomplished in a machine. So that, even in us, the spirit, or the soul, does not directly move the limbs, but only determines the course of that very subtle liquid which is called the animal spirits, which, running continually from the heart by the brain into the muscles, is the cause of all the movements of our limbs, and often may cause many different motions, one as easily as the other.

"And it does not even always exert this determination; for among the movements which take place in us, there are many which do not depend on the mind at all, such as the beating of the heart, the digestion of food, the nutrition, the respiration, of those who sleep; and, even in those who are awake, walking, singing, and other similar actions, when they are performed without the mind

* "Réponse de M. Descartes à M. Morus." 1649. "Œuvres," tome x. p. 204. "Mais le plus grand de tous les préjugés que nous ayons retenus de notre enfance, est celui de croire que les bêtes pensent" etc.

thinking about them. And, when one who falls from a height throws his hands forwards to save his head, it is in virtue of no ratiocination that he performs this action; it does not depend upon his mind, but takes place merely because his senses being affected by the present danger, some change arises in his brain which determines the animal spirits to pass thence into the nerves, in such a manner as is required to produce this motion, in the same way as in a machine, and without the mind being able to hinder it. Now since we observe this in ourselves, why should we be so much astonished if the light reflected from the body of a wolf into the eye of a sheep has the same force to excite in it the motion of flight.

"After having observed this, if we wish to learn by reasoning, whether certain movements of beasts are comparable to those which are effected in us by the operation of the mind, or, on the contrary, to those which depend only on the animal spirits and the disposition of the organs, it is necessary to consider the difference between the two, which I have explained in the fifth part of the Discourse on Method (for I do not think that any others are discoverable), and then it will easily be seen, that all the actions of beasts are similar only to those which we perform without the help of our minds. For which reason we shall be forced to conclude, that we know of the existence in them of no other principle of motion than the disposition of their organs and the continual affluence of animal spirits produced by the heat of the heart, which attenuates and subtilizes the blood; and, at the same time, we shall acknowledge that we have had no reason for assuming any other principle, except that, not having distinguished these two principles of motion, and seeing that the one, which depends only on the animal spirits and the organs, exists in beasts as well as in us, we have hastily concluded that the other, which depends on mind and on thought, was also possessed by them."

Descartes's line of argument is perfectly clear. He starts from reflex action in man, from the unquestionable fact that, in ourselves, co-ordinate, purposive, actions may take place, without the intervention of consciousness or volition, or even contrary to the latter. As actions of a certain degree of complexity are brought about by mere mechanism, why may not actions of still greater complexity be the result of a more refined mechanism? What proof is there that brutes are other than a superior race of marionettes, which eat without pleasure, cry without pain, desire nothing, know nothing, and only simulate intelligence as a bee simulates a mathematician? *

The Port Royalists adopted the hypothesis that brutes are machines, and are said to have carried its practical applications so far, as to treat domestic animals with neglect, if not with actual cruelty. As late as the middle of the eighteenth century, the problem was discussed very fully and ably by Bouillier, in his "Essai philosophique sur l'Ame des Bêtes," while Condillac deals with it in his "Traité des Animaux;" but since then it has received little attention. Nevertheless, modern research has brought to light a great multitude of facts, which not only show that Descartes's view is defensible, but render it far more defensible than it was in his day.

It must be premised, that it is wholly impossible absolutely to prove the presence or absence of consciousness in anything but one's own brain, though, by analogy, we are justified in assuming its existence in other men. Now if, by some accident, a man's spinal cord is divided, his limbs are paralyzed, so far as his volition is concerned, below the point of injury; and he is incapable of experiencing all those states of consciousness, which, in his uninjured state, would be excited by irritation of those nerves which come off below the injury. If the spinal cord is divided in the middle of the back, for example, the skin of the feet may be cut, or pinched, or burned, or wetted with vitriol, without any sensation of touch, or of pain, arising in consciousness. So far as the man is concerned, therefore, the part of the central nervous system which lies beyond the injury is cut off from consciousness. It must indeed be admitted, that, if any one think fit to maintain that the spinal cord below the injury is conscious, but that it is cut off from any means of making its consciousness known to the other consciousness in the brain, there is no means of driving him from his position by logic. But assuredly there is no way of proving it, and in the matter of consciousness, if in anything, we may hold by the rule, "De non apparentibus et de non existentibus eadem est ratio." However near the brain the

* Malebranche states the view taken by orthodox Cartesians in 1689 very forcibly: "Ainsi dans les chiens, les chats, et les autres animaux, il n'y a ny intelligence, ny âme spirituelle comme on l'entend ordinairement. Ils mangent sans plaisir; ils crient sans douleur; ils croissent sans le sçavoir; ils ne désirent rien; ils ne connoissent rien; et s'ils agissent avec adresse et d'une manière qui marque l'intelligence, c'est que Dieu les faisant pour les conserver, il a conformé leurs corps de telle manière, qu'ils évitent organiquement, sans le sçavoir, tout ce qui peut les détruire et qu'ils semblent craindre." ("Feuillet de Conches. Méditations Métaphysiques et Correspondance de N. Malebranche. Neuvième Méditation." 1841.)

spinal cord is injured, consciousness remains intact, except that the irritation of parts below the injury is no longer represented by sensation. On the other hand, pressure upon the anterior division of the brain, or extensive injuries to it, abolish consciousness. Hence, it is a highly probable conclusion, that consciousness in man depends upon the integrity of the anterior division of the brain, while the middle and hinder divisions of the brain, and the rest of the nervous centers, have nothing to do with it. And it is further highly probable, that what is true for man is true for other vertebrated animals.

We may assume, then, that in a living vertebrated animal, any segment of the cerebro-spinal axis (or spinal cord and brain) separated from that anterior division of the brain which is the organ of consciousness, is as completely incapable of giving rise to consciousness, as we know it to be incapable of carrying out volitions. Nevertheless, this separated segment of the spinal cord is not passive and inert. On the contrary, it is the seat of extremely remarkable powers. In our imaginary case of injury, the man would, as we have seen, be devoid of sensation in his legs, and would have not the least power of moving them. But, if the soles of his feet were tickled, the legs would be drawn up, just as vigorously as they would have been before the injury. We know exactly what happens when the soles of the feet are tickled; a molecular change takes place in the sensory nerves of the skin, and is propagated along them and through the posterior roots of the spinal nerves, which are constituted by them, to the gray matter of the spinal cord. Through that gray matter, the molecular motion is reflected into the anterior roots of the same nerves, constituted by the filaments which supply the muscles of the legs, and, traveling along these motor filaments, reaches the muscles, which at once contract, and cause the limbs to be drawn up.

In order to move the legs in this way, a definite co-ordination of muscular contractions is necessary; the muscles must contract in a certain order and with duly proportioned force; and moreover, as the feet are drawn away from the source of irritation, it may be said that the action has a final cause, or is purposive.

Thus it follows, that the gray matter of the segment of the man's spinal cord, though it is devoid of consciousness, nevertheless responds to a simple stimulus by giving rise to a complex set of muscular contractions, co-ordinated toward a definite end, and serving an obvious purpose.

If the spinal cord of a frog is cut across, so as to provide us with a segment separated from the brain, we shall have a subject parallel to the injured man, on which experiments can be made without remorse; as we have a right to conclude that a frog's spinal cord is not likely to be conscious when a man's is not.

Now the frog behaves just as the man did. The legs are utterly paralyzed, so far as voluntary movement is concerned; but they are vigorously drawn up to the body when any irritant is applied to the foot. But let us study our frog a little farther. Touch the skin of the side of the body with a little acetic acid, which gives rise to all the signs of great pain in an uninjured frog. In this case, there can be no pain, because the application is made to a part of the skin supplied with nerves which come off from the cord below the point of section; nevertheless, the frog lifts up the limb of the same side, and applies the foot to rub off the acetic acid; and, what is still more remarkable, if the limb be held so that the frog cannot use it, it will, by and by, move the limb of the other side, turn it across the body, and use it for the same rubbing process. It is impossible that the frog, if it were in its entirety and could reason, should perform actions more purposive than these: and yet we have most complete assurance that, in this case, the frog is not acting from purpose, has no consciousness, and is a mere insensible machine.

But now suppose that, instead of making a section of the cord in the middle of the body, it had been made in such a manner as to separate the hindermost division of the brain from the rest of the organ, and suppose the foremost two-thirds of the brain entirely taken away. The frog is then absolutely devoid of any spontaneity; it sits upright in the attitude which a frog habitually assumes; and it will not stir unless it is touched; but it differs from the frog which I have just described in this, that, if it be thrown into the water, it begins to swim, and swims just as well as the perfect frog does. But swimming requires the combination and successive co-ordination of a great number of muscular actions. And we are forced to conclude, that the impression made upon the sensory nerves of the skin of the frog by the contact with the water into which it is thrown, causes the transmission to the central nervous apparatus of an impulse, which sets going a certain machinery by which all the muscles of swimming are brought into play in due co-ordination. If the frog be stimulated by some irritating body, it jumps or walks as well as the complete frog can do. The simple sensory impression, acting through the machinery of the cord, gives rise to these complex combined movements.

It is possible to go a step farther. Suppose that only the anterior division of the brain—so much of it as lies in front of the "optic lobes"—is removed. If that operation is performed quickly and skillfully, the frog may be kept in a state of full bodily vigor for months, or it may be for years; but it will sit unmoved. It sees nothing; it hears nothing. It will starve sooner than feed itself, although food put into its mouth is swallowed. On irritation, it jumps or walks; if thrown into the water it swims. If it be put on the hand, it sits there, crouched, perfectly quiet, and would sit there forever. If the hand be inclined very gently and slowly, so that the frog would naturally tend to slip off, the creature's fore paws are shifted on to the edge of the hand, until he can just prevent himself from falling. If the turning of the hand be slowly continued, he mounts up with great care and deliberation, putting first one leg forward and then another, until he balances himself with perfect precision upon the edge; and, if the turning of the hand is continued, over he goes through the needful set of muscular operations, until he comes to be seated in security, upon the back of the hand. The doing of all this requires a delicacy of co-ordination, and a precision of adjustment of the muscular apparatus of the body, which are only comparable to those of a rope-dancer. To the ordinary influences of light, the frog, deprived of its central hemispheres, appears to be blind. Nevertheless, if the animal be put upon a table, with a book at some little distance between it and the light, and the skin of the hinder part of its body is then irritated, it will jump forward, avoiding the book by passing to the right or left of it. Although the frog, therefore, appears to have no sensation of light, visible objects act through its brain upon the motor mechanism of its body.*

It is obvious, that had Descartes been acquainted with these remarkable results of modern research, they would have furnished him with far more powerful arguments than he possessed in favor of his view of the automatism of brutes. The habits of a frog, leading its natural life, involve such simple adaptations to surrounding conditions, that the machinery which is competent to do so much without the intervention of consciousness, might well do all. And this argument is vastly strengthened by what has been learned in recent times of the marvelously complex operations which are performed mechanically, and to all appearance without consciousness, by men, when, in consequence of injury or disease, they are reduced to a condition more or less comparable to that of a frog, in which the anterior part of the brain has been removed. A case has recently been published by an eminent French physician, Dr. Mesnet, which illustrates this condition so remarkably, that I make no apology for dwelling upon it at considerable length.*

A sergeant of the French army, F——, twenty-seven years of age, was wounded during the battle of Bazeilles, by a ball which fractured his left parietal bone. He ran his bayonet through the Prussian soldier who wounded him, but almost immediately his right arm became paralyzed; after walking about two hundred yards, his right leg became similarly affected, and he lost his senses. When he recovered them, three weeks afterward, in hospital at Mayence, the right half of the body was completely paralyzed, and remained in that condition for a year. At present, the only trace of the paralysis which remains is a slight weakness of the right half of the body. Three or four months after the wound was inflicted, periodical disturbances of the functions of the brain made their appearance, and have continued ever since. The disturbances last from fifteen to thirty hours; the intervals at which they occur being from fifteen to thirty days.

For four years, therefore, the life of this man has been divided into alternating phases—short abnormal states intervening between long normal states.

* See the remarkable essay of Göltz, "Beiträge zur Lehre von den Functionen der Nervencentren des Frosches," published in 1869. I have repeated Göltz's experiments, and obtained the same results.

* "De l'Automatisme de la Mémoire et du Souvenir, dans le Somnambulisme pathologique." Par le Dr. E. Mesnet, Médecin de l'Hôpital Saint-Antoine. *L'Union Médicale*, Juillet 21 et 23, 1874. My attention was first called to a summary of this remarkable case, which appeared in the *Journal des Débats* for the 7th of August, 1874, by my friend General Strachey, F.R.S.

In the periods of normal life, the ex-sergeant's health is perfect; he is intelligent and kindly, and performs, satisfactorily, the duties of a hospital attendant. The commencement of the abnormal state is ushered in by uneasiness and a sense of weight about the forehead, which the patient compares to the constriction of a circle of iron; and, after its termination, he complains, for some hours, of dullness and heaviness of the head. But the transition from the normal to the abnormal state takes place in a few minutes, without convulsions or cries, and without anything to indicate the change to a by-stander. His movements remain free and his expression calm, except for a contraction of the brow, an incessant movement of the eyeballs, and a chewing motion of the jaws. The eyes are wide open, and their pupils dilated. If the man happens to be in a place to which he is accustomed, he walks about as usual; but if he is in a new place, or if obstacles are intentionally placed in his way, he stumbles gently against them, stops, and then, feeling over the objects with his hands, passes on one side of them. He offers no resistance to any change of direction which may be impressed upon him, or to the forcible acceleration or retardation of his movements. He eats, drinks, smokes, walks about, dresses and undresses himself, rises and goes to bed at the accustomed hours. Nevertheless, pins may be run into his body, or strong electric shocks sent through it, without causing the least indication of pain; no odorous substance, pleasant or unpleasant, makes the least impression; he eats and drinks with avidity whatever is offered, and takes asafœtida, or vinegar, or quinine, as readily as water; no noise affects him; and light influences him only under certain conditions. Dr. Mesnet remarks, that the sense of touch alone seems to persist, and indeed to be more acute and delicate than in the normal state; and it is by means of the nerves of touch, almost exclusively, that his organism is brought into relation with the external world. Here a difficulty arises. It is clear, from the facts detailed, that the nervous apparatus by which, in the normal state, sensations of touch are excited, is that by which external influences determine the movements of the body, in the abnormal state. But does the state of consciousness, which we term a tactile sensation, accompany the operation of this nervous apparatus in the abnormal state? or is consciousness utterly absent, the man being reduced to an insensible mechanism?

It is impossible to obtain direct evidence in favor of the one conclusion or the other; all that can be said is, that the case of the frog shows that man may be devoid of any kind of consciousness.

A further difficult problem is this. The man is insensible to sensory impressions made through the ear, the nose, the tongue, and, to a great extent, the eye; nor is he susceptible of pain from causes operating during his abnormal state. Nevertheless, it is possible so to act upon his tactile apparatus, as to give rise to those molecular changes in his sensorium, which are ordinarily the causes of associated trains of ideas. I give a striking example of this process in Dr. Mesnet's words:—

"Il se promenait dans le jardin, sous un massif d'arbres, on lui remet à la main sa canne qu'il avait laissé tomber quelques minutes avant. Il la palpe, promène à plusieurs reprises la main sur la poignée coudée de sa canne—devient attentif—semble prêter l'oreille—et, tout-à-coup, appelle 'Henri!' Puis, 'Les voilà! Ils sont au moins une vingtaine! à nous deux, nous en viendrons à bout!' Et alors portant la main derrière son dos comme pour prendre une cartouche, il fait le mouvement de charger son arme, se couche dans l'herbe à plat ventre, la tête cachée par un arbre, dans la position d'un tirailleur, et suit, l'arme épaulée, tous les mouvements de l'ennemi qu'il croit voir à courte distance."

In a subsequent abnormal period, Dr. Mesnet caused the patient to repeat this scene by placing him in the same conditions. Now, in this case, the question arises whether the series of actions constituting this singular pantomime was accompanied by the ordinary states of consciousness, the appropriate train of ideas, or not? Did the man dream that he was skirmishing? or was he in the condition of one of Vaucauson's automata—a senseless mechanism worked by molecular changes in his nervous system? The analogy of the frog shows that the latter assumption is perfectly justifiable.

The ex-sergeant has a good voice, and had, at one time, been employed as a singer at a café. In one of his abnormal states he was observed to begin humming a tune. He then went to his room, dressed himself carefully, and took up some parts of a periodical novel, which lay on his bed, as if he were trying to find something. Dr. Mesnet, suspecting that he was seeking his music, made up one of these into a roll and put it into his hand. He appeared satisfied, took up his cane and went down stairs to the door. Here Dr. Mesnet turned him round, and he walked quite contentedly, in the opposite direction, toward the room of the concièrge. The light of the sun shining through a window now happened to fall upon him, and seemed to suggest the footlights of the stage on which he was accustomed to make his appearance. He stopped, opened his roll of imaginary music, put himself into the attitude of a singer, and sang, with perfect execution, three songs, one after the other. After which he wiped his face with his handkerchief and drank, without a grimace, a tumbler of strong vinegar and water which was put into his hand.

An experiment which may be performed upon the frog deprived of the fore part of its brain, well known as Göltz's "Quakversuch," affords a parallel to this performance. If the skin of a certain part of the back of such a frog is gently stroked with the finger, it immediately croaks. It never croaks unless it is so stroked, and the croak always follows the stroke, just as the sound of a repeater follows the touching of the spring. In the frog, this "song" is innate—so to speak *à priori*—and depends upon a mechanism in the brain governing the vocal apparatus, which is set at work by the molecular change set up in the sensory nerves of the skin of the back by the contact of a foreign body.

In man there is also a vocal mechanism, and the cry of an infant is in the same sense innate and *à priori*, inasmuch as it depends on an organic relation between its sensory nerves and the nervous mechanism which governs the vocal apparatus. Learning to speak, and learning to sing, are processes by which the vocal mechanism is set to new tunes. A song which has been learned has its molecular equivalent, which potentially represents it in the brain, just as a musical box wound up potentially represents an overture. Touch the stop and the overture begins; send a molecular impulse along the proper afferent nerve and the singer begins his song.

Again, the manner in which the frog, though apparently insensible to light, is yet, under some circumstances, influenced by visual images, finds a singular parallel in the case of the ex-sergeant.

Sitting at a table, in one of his abnormal states, he took up a pen, felt for paper and ink, and began to write a letter to his general, in which he recommended himself for a medal, on account of his good conduct, and courage. It occurred to Dr. Mesnet to ascertain experimentally how far vision was concerned in this act of writing. He therefore interposed a screen between the man's eyes and his hands; under these circumstances he went on writing for a short time, but the words became illegible, and he finally stopped, without manifesting any discontent. On the withdrawal of the screen he began to write again where he had left off. The substitution of water for ink in the inkstand had a similar result. He stopped, looked at his pen, wiped it on his coat, dipped it in the water, and began again, with the same effect.

On one occasion, he began to write upon the topmost of ten superimposed sheets of paper. After he had written a line or two, this sheet was suddenly drawn away. There was a slight expression of surprise, but he continued his letter on the second sheet exactly as if it had been the first. This operation was repeated five times, so that the fifth sheet contained nothing but the writer's signature at the bottom of the page. Nevertheless, when the signature was finished his eyes turned to the top of the blank sheet, and he went through the form of reading over what he had written, a movement of the lips accompanying each word; moreover, with his pen, he put in such corrections as were needed, in that part of the blank page which corresponded with the position of the words which required correction, in the sheets which had been taken away. If the five sheets had been transparent, therefore, they would, when superposed, have formed a properly written and corrected letter.

Immediately after he had written his letter, F—— got up, walked down to the garden, made himself a cigarette, lighted and smoked it. He was about to prepare another, but sought in vain for his tobacco-pouch, which had been purposely taken away. The pouch was now thrust before his eyes and put under his nose, but he neither saw nor smelt it; but, when it was placed in his hand, he at once seized it, made a fresh cigarette, and ignited a match to light the latter. The match was blown out and another lighted match placed close before his eyes, but he made no attempt to take it; and, if his cigarette was lighted for him, he made no attempt to smoke. All this time the eyes were vacant, and neither winked, nor exhibited any contraction of the pupils. From these and other experiments, Dr. Mesnet draws the conclusion that his patient sees some things and not others; that the sense of sight is accessible to all things which are brought into relation with him by the sense of touch, and, on the contrary, insensible to things which lie outside this relation. He sees the match he holds, and does not see any other.

Just so the frog "sees" the book which is in the way of his jump, at the same time that isolated visual impressions take no effect upon him.*

As I have pointed out, it is impossible to prove that F—— is absolutely unconscious in his abnormal state, but it is no less impossible to prove the contrary; and the case of the frog goes a long way to justify the assumption that, in the abnormal state, the man is a mere insensible machine.

If such facts as these had come under the knowledge of Descartes, would they not have formed an apt commentary upon that remarkable passage in the "Traité de l'Homme," which I have quoted elsewhere,† but which is worth repetition?—

"All the functions which I have attributed to this machine (the body), as the digestion of food, the pulsation of the heart and of the arteries; the nutrition and the growth of the limbs; respiration, wakefulness, and sleep; the reception of light, sounds, odors, flavors, heat, and such like qualities, in the organs of the external senses; the impression of the ideas of these in the organ of common sensation and in the imagination; the retention or the impression of these ideas on the memory; the internal movements of the appetites and the passions; and lastly, the external movements of all the limbs, which follow so aptly, as well the action of the objects which are presented to the senses, as the impressions which meet in the memory, that they imitate as nearly as possible those of a real man; I desire, I say, that you should consider that these functions in the machine naturally proceed from the mere arrangement of its organs, neither more nor less than do the movements of a clock, or other automaton, from that of its weights and its wheels; so that, so far as these are concerned, it is not necessary to conceive any other vegetative or sensitive soul, nor any other principle of motion or of life, than the blood and the spirits agitated by the fire which burns continually in the heart, and which is no wise essentially different from all the fires which exist in inanimate bodies."

And would Descartes not have been justified in asking why we need deny that animals are machines, when men, in a state of unconsciousness, perform, mechanically, actions as complicated and as seemingly rational as those of any animals?

But though I do not think that Descartes's hypothesis can be positively refuted, I am not disposed to accept it. The doctrine of continuity is too well established for it to be permissible to me to suppose that any complex natural phenomenon comes into existence suddenly, and without being preceded by simpler modifications; and very strong arguments would be needed to prove that such complex phenomena, as those of consciousness, first make their appearance in man. We know, that, in the individual man, consciousness grows from a dim glimmer to its full light, whether we consider the infant advancing in years, or the adult emerging from slumber and swoon. We know, further, that the lower animals possess, though less developed, that part of the brain which we have every reason to believe to be the organ of consciousness in man; and as, in other cases, function and organ are proportional, so we have a right to conclude it is with the brain; and that the brutes, though they may not possess our intensity of consciousness, and though, from the absence of language, they can have no trains of thoughts, but only trains of feelings, yet have a consciousness which, more or less distinctly, foreshadows our own.

I confess that, in view of the struggle

* Those who have had occasion to become acquainted with the phenomena of somnambulism and of mesmerism, will be struck with the close parallel which they present to the proceedings of F. in his abnormal state. But the great value of Dr. Mesnet's observations lies in the fact that the abnormal condition is traceable to a definite injury to the brain, and that the circumstances are such as to keep us clear of the cloud of voluntary and involuntary fictions in which the truth is too often smothered in such cases. In the unfortunate subjects of such abnormal conditions of the brain, the disturbance of the sensory and intellectual faculties is not unfrequently accompanied by a perturbation of the moral nature, which may manifest itself in a most astonishing love of lying for its own sake. And, in this respect, also, F.'s case is singularly instructive, for though, in his normal state, he is a perfectly honest man, in his abnormal condition he is an inveterate thief, stealing and hiding away whatever he can lay hands on, with much dexterity, and with an absurd indifference as to whether the property is his own or not. Hoffman's terrible conception of the "Doppeltgänger" is realized by men in this state—who live two lives, in the one of which they may be guilty of the most criminal acts, while, in the other, they are eminently virtuous and respectable. Neither life knows anything of the other. Dr. Mesnet states that he has watched a man in his abnormal state elaborately prepare to hang himself, and has let him go on until asphyxia set in, when he cut him down. But on passing into the normal state the would-be suicide was wholly ignorant of what had happened. The problem of responsibility is here as complicated as that of the prince-bishop, who swore as a prince and not as a bishop. "But, highness, if the prince is damned what will become of the bishop?" said the peasant.

† "Lay Sermons, Essays and Reviews," p. 355.

for existence which goes on in the animal world, and of the frightful quantity of pain with which it must be accompanied, I should be glad if the probabilities were in favor of Descartes's hypothesis; but, on the other hand, considering the terrible practical consequences to domestic animals which might ensue from any error on our part, it is as well to err on the right side, if we err at all, and deal with them as weaker brethren, who are bound, like the rest of us, to pay their toll for living, and suffer what is needful for the general good. As Hartley finely says, "We seem to be in the place of God to them;" and we may justly follow the precedents He sets in nature in our dealings with them.

But though we may see reason to disagree with Descartes's hypothesis that brutes are unconscious machines, it does not follow that he was wrong in regarding them as automata. They may be more or less conscious, sensitive, automata; and the view that they are such conscious machines is that which is implicitly, or explicitly, adopted by most persons. When we speak of the actions of the lower animals being guided by instinct and not by reason, what we really mean is that, though they feel as we do, yet their actions are the results of their physical organization. We believe, in short, that they are machines, one part of which (the nervous system) not only sets the rest in motion, and co-ordinates its movements in relation with changes in surrounding bodies, but is provided with special apparatus, the function of which is the calling into existence of those states of consciousness which are termed sensations, emotions, and ideas. I believe that this generally accepted view is the best expression of the facts at present known.

It is experimentally demonstrable—any one who cares to run a pin into himself may perform a sufficient demonstration of the fact—that a mode of motion of the nervous system is the immediate antecedent of a state of consciousness. All but the adherents of "Occasionalism," or of the doctrine of "Pre-established Harmony" (if any such now exist), must admit that we have as much reason for regarding the mode of motion of the nervous system as the cause of the state of consciousness, as we have for regarding any event as the cause of another. How the one phenomenon causes the other we know, as much or as little, as in any other case of causation; but we have as much right to believe that the sensation is an effect of the molecular change, as we have to believe that motion is an effect of impact; and there is as much propriety in saying that the brain evolves sensation, as there is in saying that an iron rod, when hammered, evolves heat.

As I have endeavored to show, we are justified in supposing that something analogous to what happens in ourselves takes place in the brutes, and that the affections of their sensory nerves give rise to molecular changes in the brain, which again give rise to, or evolve, the corresponding states of consciousness. Nor can there be any reasonable doubt that the emotions of brutes, and such ideas as they possess, are similarly dependent upon molecular brain changes. Each sensory impression leaves behind a record in the structure of the brain—an "ideagenous" molecule, so to speak, which is competent, under certain conditions, to reproduce, in a fainter condition, the state of consciousness which corresponds with that sensory impression; and it is these "ideagenous molecules" which are the physical basis of memory.

It may be assumed, then, that molecular changes in the brain are the causes of all the states of consciousness of brutes. Is there any evidence that these states of consciousness may, conversely, cause those molecular changes which give rise to muscular motion? I see no such evidence. The frog walks, hops, swims, and goes through his gymnastic performances quite as well without consciousness, and consequently without volition, as with it; and, if a frog, in his natural state, possesses anything corresponding with what we call volition, there is no reason to think that it is anything but a concomitant of the molecular changes in the brain which form part of the series involved in the production of motion.

The consciousness of brutes would appear to be related to the mechanism of their body simply as a collateral product of its working, and to be as completely without any power of modifying that working as the steam-whistle which accompanies the work of a locomotive engine is without influence upon its machinery. Their volition, if they have any, is an emotion indicative of physical changes, not a cause of such changes.

This conception of the relations of states of consciousness with molecular changes in the brain—of *psychoses* with *neuroses*—does not prevent us from ascribing free will to brutes. For an agent is free when there is nothing to prevent him from doing that which he desires to do. If a grayhound chases a hare, he is a free agent, because his action is in entire accordance with his strong desire to catch the hare; while so long as he is held back by the leash he is not free, being prevented by external force from following his inclination. And the ascription of freedom to the grayhound under the former circumstances is by no means inconsistent with the other aspect of the facts of the case—that he is a machine impelled to the chase, and caused, at the same time, to have the desire to catch the game by the impression which the rays of light proceeding from the hare make upon his eyes, and through them upon his brain.

Much ingenious argument has, at various times, been bestowed upon the question: How is it possible to imagine that volition, which is a state of consciousness, and, as such, has not the slightest community of nature with matter in motion, can act upon the moving matter of which the body is composed, as it is assumed to do in voluntary acts? But if, as is here suggested, the voluntary acts of brutes—or, in other words, the acts which they desire to perform—are as purely mechanical as the rest of their actions, and are simply accompanied by the state of consciousness called volition, the inquiry, so far as they are concerned, becomes superfluous. Their volitions do not enter into the chain of causation of their actions at all.

The hypothesis that brutes are conscious automata is perfectly consistent with any view that may be held respecting the often discussed and curious question whether they have souls or not; and, if they have souls, whether those souls are immortal or not. It is obviously harmonious with the most literal adherence to the text of Scripture concerning "the beast that perisheth;" but it is not inconsistent with the amiable conviction ascribed by Pope to his "untutored savage," that when he passes to the happy hunting-grounds in the sky, "his faithful dog shall bear him company." If the brutes have consciousness and no souls, then it is clear that, in them, consciousness is a direct function of material changes; while, if they possess immaterial subjects of consciousness or souls, then, as consciousness is brought into existence only as the consequence of molecular motion of the brain, it follows that it is an indirect product of material changes. The soul stands related to the body as the bell of a clock to the works, and consciousness answers to the sound which the bell gives out when it is struck.

Thus far I have strictly confined myself to the problem with which I proposed to deal at starting—the automatism of brutes. The question is, I believe, a perfectly open one, and I feel happy in running no risk of either Papal or Presbyterian condemnation for the views which I have ventured to put forward. And there are so very few interesting questions which one is, at present, allowed to think out scientifically—to go as far as reason leads, and stop where evidence comes to an end—without speedily being deafened by the tattoo of "the drum ecclesiastic"—that I have luxuriated in my rare freedom, and would now willingly bring this disquisition to an end if I could hope that other people would go no farther. Unfortunately, past experience debars me from entertaining any such hope, even if

> ". . . . . that drum's discordant sound
> Parading round and round and round,"

were not, at present, as audible to me, as it was to the mild poet who ventured to express his hatred of drums in general, in that well-known couplet.

It will be said, that I mean that the conclusions deduced from the study of the brutes are applicable to man, and that the logical consequences of such application are fatalism, materialism, and atheism—whereupon the drums will beat the *pas de charge*.

One does not do battle with drummers; but I venture to offer a few remarks for the calm consideration of thoughtful persons, untrammeled by foregone conclusions, unpledged to shore-up tottering dogmas, and anxious only to know the true bearings of the case.

It is quite true that, to the best of my judgment, the argumentation which applies to brutes holds equally good of men; and, therefore, that all states of consciousness in us, as in them, are immediately caused by molecular changes of the brain-substance. It seems to me that in men, as in brutes, there is no proof that any state of consciousness is the cause of change in the motion of the matter of the organism. If these positions are well based, it follows that our mental conditions are simply the symbols in consciousness of the changes which take place automatically in the organism; and that, to take an extreme illustration, the feeling we call volition is not the cause of a voluntary act, but the symbol of that state of the brain which is the immediate cause of that act. We are conscious automata, endowed with free will in the only intelligible sense of that much-abused term—inasmuch as in many respects we are able to do as we like—but none the less parts of the great series of causes and effects which, in unbroken continuity, composes that which is, and has been, and shall be—the sum of existence.

As to the logical consequences of this conviction of mine, I may be permitted to remark that logical consequences are the scarecrows of fools and the beacons of wise men. The only question which any wise man can ask himself, and which any honest man will ask himself, is whether a doctrine is true or false. Consequences will take care of themselves; at most their importance can only justify us in testing with extra care the reasoning process from which they result.

So that if the view I have taken did really and logically lead to fatalism, materialism, and atheism, I should profess myself a fatalist, materialist, and atheist; and I should look upon those who, while they believed in my honesty of purpose and intellectual competency, should raise a hue and cry against me, as people who by their own admission preferred lying to truth, and whose opinions therefore were unworthy of the smallest attention.

But, as I have endeavored to explain on other occasions, I really have no claim to rank myself among fatalistic, materialistic, or atheistic philosophers. Not among fatalists, for I take the conception of necessity to have a logical, and not a physical foundation; not among materialists, for I am utterly incapable of conceiving the existence of matter if there is no mind in which to picture that existence; not among atheists, for the problem of the ultimate cause of existence is one which seems to me to be hopelessly out of reach of my poor powers. Of all the senseless babble I have ever had occasion to read, the demonstrations of these philosophers who undertake to tell us all about the nature of God would be the worst, if they were not surpassed by the still greater absurdities of the philosophers who try to prove that there is no God.

And if this personal disclaimer should not be enough, let me further point out that a great many persons whose acuteness and learning will not be contested, and whose Christian piety, and, in some cases, strict orthodoxy, are above suspicion, have held more or less definitely the view that man is a conscious automaton.

It is held, for example, in substance, by the whole school of predestinarian theologians, typified by St. Augustine, Calvin, and Jonathan Edwards—the great work of the latter on the will showing in this, as in other cases, that the growth of physical science has introduced no new difficulties of principle into theological problems, but has merely given visible body, as it were, to those which already existed.

Among philosophers, the pious Geulincx and the whole school of occasionalist Cartesians held this view: the orthodox Leibnitz invented the term "automate spirituel," and applied it to man; the fervent Christian, Hartley, was one of the chief advocates and best expositors of the doctrine; while another zealous apologist of Christianity in a sceptical age, and a contemporary of Hartley, Charles Bonnet, the Genevese naturalist, has embodied the doctrine in language of such precision and simplicity, that I will quote the little-known passage of his "Essai de Psychologie" at length:—

"ANOTHER HYPOTHESIS CONCERNING THE MECHANISM OF IDEAS.*

"Philosophers accustomed to judge of things by that which they are in themselves, and not by their relation to receive ideas, would not be shocked if they met with the proposition that the soul is a mere spectator of the movements of its body: that the latter performs of itself all that series of actions which constitutes life: that it moves of itself: that it is the body alone which reproduces ideas, compares and arranges them; which forms reasonings, imagines and executes plans of all kinds, etc. This hypothesis, though perhaps of an excessive boldness, nevertheless deserves some consideration.

"It is not to be denied that Supreme Power could create an automaton which should exactly imitate all the external and internal actions of man.

"I understand by external actions, all those movements which pass under our eyes; I term internal actions, all the motions which in the natural state cannot be observed because they take place in the interior of the body—such as the movements of digestion, circulation, sensation, etc. Moreover, I include in this category the movements which give rise to ideas, whatever be their nature.

"In the automaton which we are considering everything would be precisely determined. Everything would occur according to the rules of the most admirable mechanism: one state would succeed another state, one operation would lead to another operation, according to invariable laws; motion would become

* "Essai de Psychologie," chap. xxvii.

alternately cause and effect, effect and cause; reaction would answer to action, and reproduction to production.

"Constructed with definite relations to the activity of the beings which compose the world, the automaton would receive impressions from it, and, in faithful correspondence thereto, it would execute a corresponding series of motions.

"Indifferent toward any determination, it would yield equally to all, if the first impressions did not, so to speak, wind up the machine and decide its operations and its course.

"The series of movements which this automaton could execute would distinguish it from all others formed on the same model, but which, not having been placed in similar circumstances, would not have experienced the same impressions, or would not have experienced them in the same order.

"The senses of the automaton, set in motion by the objects presented to it, would communicate their motion to the brain, the chief motor apparatus of the machine. This would put in action the muscles of the hands and feet, in virtue of their secret connection with the senses. These muscles, alternately contracted and dilated, would approximate or remove the automaton from the objects, in the relation which they would bear to the conservation or the destruction of the machine.

"The motions of perception and sensation which the objects would have impressed on the brain, would be preserved in it by the energy of its mechanism. They would become more vivid according to the actual condition of the automaton, considered in itself and relatively to the objects.

"Words being only the motions impressed on the organ of hearing and that of voice, the diversity of these movements, their combination, the order in which they would succeed one another, would represent judgments, reasoning, and all the operations of the mind.

"A close correspondence between the organs of the senses, either by the opening into one another of their nervous ramifications, or by interposed springs (*ressorts*), would establish such a connection in their working, that, on the occasion of the movements impressed on one of these organs, other movements would be excited, or would become more vivid in some of the other senses.

"Give the automaton a soul which contemplates its movements, which believes itself to be the author of them, which has different volitions on the occasion of the different movements, and you will on this hypothesis construct a man.

"But would this man be free? Can the feeling of our liberty, this feeling which is so clear and so distinct and so vivid as to persuade us that we are the authors of our actions, be conciliated with this hypothesis? If it removes the difficulty which attends the conception of the action of the soul on the body, on the other hand it leaves untouched that which meets us in endeavoring to conceive the action of the body on the soul."

But if Leibnitz, Jonathan Edwards, and Hartley—men who rank among the giants of the world of thought—could see no antagonism between the doctrine under discussion and Christian orthodoxy, is it not just possible that smaller folk may be wrong in making such a coil about "logical consequences"? And seeing how large a share of this clamor is raised by the clergy of one denomination or another, may I say, in conclusion, that it really would be well if ecclesiastical persons would reflect that ordination, whatever deep-seated graces it may confer, has never been observed to be followed by any visible increase in the learning or the logic of its subject. Making a man a Bishop, or entrusting him with the office of ministering to even the largest of Presbyterian congregations, or setting him up to lecture to a Church congress, really does not in the smallest degree augment such title to respect as his opinions may intrinsically possess. And, when such a man presumes on an authority which was conferred upon him for other purposes, to sit in judgment upon matters his incompetence to deal with which is patent, it is permissible to ignore his sacerdotal pretensions, and to tell him, as one would tell a mere common, unconsecrated layman, that it is not necessary for any man to occupy himself with problems of this kind unless he so choose; life is filled full enough by the performance of its ordinary and obvious duties. But that, if a man elect to become a judge of these grave questions; still more, if he assume the responsibility of attaching praise or blame to his fellowmen for the conclusions at which they arrive touching them, he will commit a sin more grievous than most breaches of the Decalogue, unless he avoid a lazy reliance upon the information that is gathered by prejudice and filtered through passion, unless he go back to the prime sources of knowledge—the facts of nature, and the thoughts of those wise men who for generations past have been her best interpreters.

II.

SCIENCE AND CULTURE.*

SIX years ago, as some of my present hearers may remember, I had the privi-

* An Address delivered at the opening of Sir Josiah Mason's Science College, Birmingham (1880).

lege of addressing a large assemblage of the inhabitants of this city, who had gathered together to do honor to the memory of their famous townsman, Joseph Priestley; and, if any satisfaction attaches to posthumous glory, we may hope that the manes of the burnt-out philosopher were then finally appeased.

No man, however, who is endowed with a fair share of common sense, and not more than a fair share of vanity, will identify either contemporary or posthumous fame with the highest good; and Priestley's life leaves no doubt that he, at any rate, set a much higher value upon the advancement of knowledge, and the promotion of that freedom of thought which is at once the cause and the consequence of intellectual progress.

Hence I am disposed to think that, if Priestley could be amongst us to-day, the occasion of our meeting would afford him even greater pleasure than the proceedings which celebrated the centenary of his chief discovery. The kindly heart would be moved, the high sense of social duty would be satisfied, by the spectacle of well-earned wealth, neither squandered in tawdry luxury and vainglorious show, nor scattered with the careless charity which blesses neither him that gives nor him that takes, but expended in the execution of a well-considered plan for the aid of present and future generations of those who are willing to help themselves.

We shall all be of one mind thus far. But it is needful to share Priestley's keen interest in physical science; and to have learned, as he had learned, the value of scientific training in fields of inquiry apparently far remote from physical science; in order to appreciate, as he would have appreciated, the value of the noble gift which Sir Josiah Mason has bestowed upon the inhabitants of the Midland district.

For us children of the nineteenth century, however, the establishment of a college under the conditions of Sir Josiah Mason's Trust, has a significance apart from any which it could have possessed a hundred years ago. It appears to be an indication that we are reaching the crisis of the battle, or rather of the long series of battles, which have been fought over education in a campaign which began long before Priestley's time, and will probably not be finished just yet.

In the last century, the combatants were the champions of ancient literature, on the one side, and those of modern literature on the other; but, some thirty years* ago, the contest became complicated by the appearance of a third army, ranged round the banner of Physical Science.

I am not aware that any one has authority to speak in the name of this new host. For it must be admitted to be somewhat of a guerilla force, composed largely of irregulars, each of whom fights pretty much for his own hand. But the impressions of a full private, who has seen a good deal of service in the ranks, respecting the present position of affairs and the conditions of a permanent peace, may not be devoid of interest; and I do not know that I could make a better use of the present opportunity than by laying them before you.

From the time that the first suggestion to introduce physical science into ordinary education was timidly whispered, until now, the advocates of scientific education have met with opposition of two kinds. On the one hand, they have been pooh-poohed by the men of business who pride themselves on being the representatives of practicality; while, on the other hand, they have been excommunicated by the classical scholars, in their capacity of Levites in charge of the ark of culture and monopolists of liberal education.

The practical men believed that the idol whom they worship—rule of thumb—has been the source of the past prosperity, and will suffice for the future welfare of the arts and manufactures. They were of opinion that science is speculative rubbish; that theory and practice have nothing to do with one another; and that the scientific habit of mind is an impediment, rather than an aid, in the conduct of ordinary affairs.

I have used the past tense in speaking of the practical men—for although they were very formidable thirty years ago, I am not sure that the pure species has not been extirpated. In fact, so far as mere argument goes, they have been subjected to such a *feu d'enfer* that it is a miracle if any have escaped. But I have remarked that your typical practical man has an unexpected resemblance to one of Milton's angels. His spiritual wounds, such as are inflicted by logical weapons, may be as deep as a well and as wide as a church door, but beyond shedding a few drops of ichor, celestial or otherwise, he is no

* The advocacy of the introduction of physical science into general education by George Combe and others commenced a good deal earlier; but the movement had acquired hardly any practical force before the time to which I refer.

whit the worse. So, if any of these opponents be left, I will not waste time in vain repetition of the demonstrative evidence of the practical value of science; but knowing that a parable will sometimes penetrate where syllogisms fail to effect an entrance, I will offer a story for their consideration.

Once upon a time, a boy, with nothing to depend upon but his own vigorous nature, was thrown into the thick of the struggle for existence in the midst of a great manufacturing population. He seems to have had a hard fight, inasmuch as, by the time he was thirty years of age, his total disposable funds amounted to twenty pounds. Nevertheless, middle life found him giving proof of his comprehension of the practical problems he had been roughly called upon to solve, by a career of remarkable prosperity.

Finally, having reached old age with its well-earned surroundings of "honor, troops of friends," the hero of my story bethought himself of those who were making a like start in life, and how he could stretch out a helping hand to them.

After long and anxious reflection this successful practical man of business could devise nothing better than to provide them with the means of obtaining "sound, extensive, and practical scientific knowledge." And he devoted a large part of his wealth and five years of incessant work to this end.

I need not point the moral of a tale which, as the solid and spacious fabric of the Scientific College assures us, is no fable, nor can anything which I could say intensify the force of this practical answer to practical objections.

We may take it for granted then, that, in the opinion of those best qualified to judge, the diffusion of thorough scientific education is an absolutely essential condition of industrial progress; and that the College which has been opened today will confer an inestimable boon upon those whose livelihood is to be gained by the practice of the arts and manufactures of the district.

The only question worth discussion is, whether the conditions, under which the work of the College is to be carried out, are such as to give it the best possible chance of achieving permanent success.

Sir Josiah Mason, without doubt most wisely, has left very large freedom of action to the trustees, to whom he proposes ultimately to commit the administration of the College, so that they may be able to adjust its arrangements in accordance with the changing conditions of the future. But, with respect to three points, he has laid most explicit injunctions upon both administrators and teachers.

Party politics are forbidden to enter into the minds of either, so far as the work of the College is concerned; theology is as sternly banished from its precincts; and finally, it is especially declared that the College shall make no provision for "mere literary instruction and education."

It does not concern me at present to dwell upon the first two injunctions any longer than may be needful to express my full conviction of their wisdom. But the third prohibition brings us face to face with those other opponents of scientific education, who are by no means in the moribund condition of the practical man, but alive, alert, and formidable.

It is not impossible that we shall hear this express exclusion of "literary instruction and education" from a College which, nevertheless, professes to give a high and efficient education, sharply criticised. Certainly the time was that the Levites of culture would have sounded their trumpets against its walls as against an educational Jericho.

How often have we not been told that the study of physical science is incompetent to confer culture; that it touches none of the higher problems of life; and, what is worse, that the continual devotion to scientific studies tends to generate a narrow and bigoted belief in the applicability of scientific methods to the search after truth of all kinds. How frequently one has reason to observe that no reply to a troublesome argument tells so well as calling its author a "mere scientific specialist." And, as I am afraid it is not permissible to speak of this form of opposition to scientific education in the past tense; may we not expect to be told that this, not only omission, but prohibition, of "mere literary instruction and education" is a patent example of scientific narrow-mindedness?

I am not acquainted with Sir Josiah Mason's reasons for the action which he has taken; but if, as I apprehend is the case, he refers to the ordinary classical course of our schools and universities by the name of "mere literary instruction and education," I venture to offer sundry reasons of my own in support of that action.

For I hold very strongly by two convictions—The first is, that neither the discipline nor the subject-matter of classical education is of such direct value to the student of physical science as to justify the expenditure of valuable time upon either; and the second is, that for the purpose of attaining real culture, an exclusively scientific education is at least as effectual an an exclusively literary education.

I need hardly point out to you that these opinions, especially the later, are diametrically opposed to those of the great majority of educated Englishmen, influenced as they are by school and university traditions. In their belief, culture is obtainable only by a liberal education; and a liberal education is synonymous, not merely with education and instruction in literature, but in one particular form of literature, namely, that of Greek and Roman antiquity. They hold that the man who has learned Latin and Greek, however little, is educated; while he who is versed in other branches of knowledge, however deeply, is a more or less respectable specialist, not admissible into the cultured caste. The stamp of the educated man, the University degree, is not for him.

I am too well acquainted with the generous catholicity of spirit, the true sympathy with scientific thought, which pervades the writings of our chief apostle of culture to identify him with these opinions; and yet one may cull from one and another of those epistles to the Philistines, which so much delight all who do not answer to that name, sentences which lend them some support.

Mr. Arnold tells us that the meaning of culture is "to know the best that has been thought and said in the world." It is the criticism of life contained in literature. That criticism regards "Europe as being, for intellectual and spiritual purposes, one great confederation, bound to a joint action and working to a common result; and whose members have, for their common outfit, a knowledge of Greek, Roman, and Eastern antiquity, and of one another. Special, local, and temporary advantages being put out of account, that modern nation will in the intellectual and spiritual sphere make most progress, which most thoroughly carries out this programme. And what is that but saying that we too, all of us, as individuals, the more thoroughly we carry it out, shall make the more progress?"

We have here to deal with two distinct propositions. The first, that a criticism of life is the essence of culture; the second, that literature contains the materials which suffice for the construction of such a criticism.

I think that we must all assent to the first proposition. For culture certainly means something quite different from learning or technical skill. It implies the possession of an ideal, and the habit of critically estimating the value of things by comparison with a theoretic standard. Perfect culture should apply a complete theory of life, based upon a clear knowledge alike of its possibilities and of its limitations.

But we may agree to all this, and yet strongly dissent from the assumption that literature alone is competent to supply this knowledge. After having learnt all that Greek, Roman, and Eastern antiquity have thought and said, and all that modern literatures have to tell us, it is not self-evident that we have laid a sufficiently broad and deep foundation for that criticism of life wich constitutes culture.

Indeed, to any one acquainted with the scope of physical science, it is not at all evident. Considering progress only in the "intellectual and spiritual sphere," I find myself wholly unable to admit that either nations or individuals will really advance, if their common outfit draws nothing from the stores of physical science. I should say that an army, without weapons of precision, and with no particular base of operations, might more hopefully enter upon a campaign on the Rhine, than a man, devoid of a knowledge of what physical science has done in the last century, upon a criticism of life.

When a biologist meets with an anomaly, he instinctively turns to the study of development to clear it up. The rationale of contradictory opinions may with equal confidence be sought in history.

It is, happily, no new thing that Englishmen should employ their wealth in building and endowing institutions for educational purposes. But, five or six hundred years ago, deeds of foundation expressed or implied conditions as nearly as possible contrary to those which have been thought expedient by Sir Josiah Mason. That is to say, physical science was practically ignored, while a certain literary training was enjoined as a means to the acquirement of knowledge which was essentially theological.

The reason of this singular contradiction between the actions of men alike animated by a strong and disinterested desire to promote the welfare of their fellows, is easily discovered.

At that time, in fact, if any one desired knowledge beyond such as could be obtained by his own observation, or by common conversation, his first necessity was the learn the Latin language, inasmuch as all the higher knowledge of the western world was contained in works written in that language. Hence, Latin grammar, with logic and rhetoric, studied through Latin, were the fundamentals of education. With respect to the substance of the knowledge imparted through this channel, the Jewish and Christian Scriptures, as interpreted and supplemented by the Romish Church, were held to contain a complete and infallibly true body of information.

Theological dicta were, to the thinkers of those days, that which the axioms and definitions of Euclid are to the geometers of these. The business of the philosophers of the middle ages was to deduce from the data furnished by the theolgians, conclusions in accordance with ecclesiastical decrees. They were allowed the high privilege of showing, by logical process, how and why that which the Church said was true, must be true. And if their demonstrations fell short of or exceeded this limit, the Church was maternally ready to check their aberrations, if need be, by the help of the secular arm.

Between the two, our ancestors were furnished with a compact and complete criticism of life. They were told how the world began, and how it would end; they learned that all material existence was but a base and insignificant blot upon the fair face of the spiritual world, and that nature was, to all intents and purposes, the play-ground of the devil; they learned that the earth is the center of the visible universe, and that man is the cynosure of things terrestrial; and more especially is it inculcated that the course of nature had no fixed order, but that it could be, and constantly was, altered by the agency of innumerable spiritual beings, good and bad, according as they were moved by the deeds and prayers of men. The sum and substance of the whole doctrine was to produce the conviction that the only thing really worth knowing in this world was how to secure that place in a better which, under certain conditions, the Church promised.

Our ancestors had a living belief in this theory of life, and acted upon it in their dealings with education, as in all other matters. Culture meant saintliness —after the fashion of the saints of those days; the education that led to it was, of necessity, theological; and the way to theology lay through Latin.

That the study of nature—further than was requisite for the satisfaction of every-day wants—should have any bearing on human life was far from the thoughts of men thus trained. Indeed, as nature had been cursed for man's sake, it was an obvious conclusion that those who meddled with nature were likely to come into pretty close contact with Satan. And, if any born scientific investigator followed his instincts, he might safely reckon upon earning the reputation, and probably upon suffering the fate, of a sorcerer.

Had the western world been left to itself in Chinese isolation, there is no saying how long this state of things might have endured. But, happily, it was not left to itself. Even earlier than the thirteenth century, the development of Moorish civilization in Spain and the great movement of the Crusades had introduced the leaven which, from that day to this, has never ceased to work. At first, though the intermediation of Arabic translations, afterward by the study of the originals, the western nations of Europe became acquainted with the writings of the ancient philosophers and poets, and, in time, with the whole of the vast literature of antiquity.

Whatever there was of high intellectual aspiration or dominant capacity in Italy, France, Germany, and England, spent itself for centuries in taking possession of the rich inheritance left by the dead civilizations of Greece and Rome. Marvelously aided by the invention of printing, classical learning spread and flourished. Those who possessed it prided themselves on having attained the highest culture then within the reach of mankind.

And justly. For, saving Dante on his solitary pinnacle, there was no figure in modern literature at the time of the Renascence to compare with the men of antiquity; there was no art to compete with their sculpture; there was no physical science but that which Greece had created. Above all, there was no other example of perfect intellectual freedom—of the unhesitating acceptance of reason as the sole guide to truth and the supreme arbiter of conduct.

The new learning necessarily soon exerted a profound influence upon education. The language of the monks and schoolmen seemed little better than gibberish to scholars fresh from Virgil and Cicero, and the study of Latin was placed upon a new foundation. Moreover, Latin itself ceased to afford the sole key to knowledge. The student who sought the highest thought of antiquity, found only a second-hand reflection of it in Roman literature, and turned his face to the full light of the Greeks. And after a battle, not altogether dissimilar to that which is at present being fought over the teaching of physical science, the study of Greek was recognized as an essential element of all higher education.

Thus the Humanists, as they were called, won the day; and the great reform which they effected was of incalculable service to mankind. But the Nemesis of all reformers is finality; and the reformers of education, like those of religion, fell into the profound, however common, error of mistaking the beginning for the end of the work of reformation.

The representatives of the Humanists in the nineteenth century, take their stand upon classical education as the sole avenue to culture, as firmly as if we were still in the age of Renascence. Yet, surely, the present intellectual relations of the modern and the ancient worlds are profoundly different from those which obtained three centuries ago. Leaving aside the existence of a great and characteristically modern literature, of modern painting, and, especially, of modern music, there is one feature of the present state of the civilized world which separates it more widely from the Renascence, than the Renascence was separated from the middle ages.

This distinctive character of our own times lies in the vast and constantly increasing part which is played by natural knowledge. Not only is our daily life shaped by it, not only does the prosperity of millions of men depend upon it, but our whole theory of life has long been influenced, consciously or unconsciously, by the general conceptions of the universe, which have been forced upon us by physical science.

In fact, the most elementary acquaintance with the results of scientific investigation shows us that they offer a broad and striking contradiction to the opinions so implicitly credited and taught in the middle ages.

The notions of the beginning and the end of the world entertained by our forefathers are no longer credible. It is very certain that the earth is not the chief body in the material universe, and that the world is not subordinated to man's use. It is even more certain that nature is the expression of a definite order with which nothing interferes, and that the chief business of mankind is to learn that order and govern themselves accordingly. Moreover this scientific "criticism of life" presents itself to us with different credentials from any other. It appeals not to authority, nor to what anybody may have thought or said, but to nature. It admits that all our interpretations of natural fact or more or less imperfect and symbolic, and bids the learner seek for truth not among words but among things. It warns us that the assertion which outstrips evidence is not only a blunder but a crime.

The purely classical education advocated by the representatives of the Humanists in our day, gives no inkling of all this. A man may be a better scholar than Erasmus, and know no more of the chief causes of the present intellectual fermentation than Erasmus did. Scholarly and pious persons, worthy of all respect, favor us with allocutions upon the sadness of the antagonism of science to their mediæval way of thinking, which betray an ignorance of the first principles of scientific investigation, an incapacity for understanding what a man of science means by veracity, and an unconsciousness of the weight of established scientific truths, which is almost comical.

There is no great force in the *tu quoque* argument, or else the advocates of scientific education might fairly enough retort upon the modern Humanists that they may be learned specialists, but that they possess no such sound foundation for a criticism of life as deserves the name of culture. And, indeed, if we were disposed to be cruel, we might urge that the Humanists have brought this reproach upon themselves, not because they are too full of the spirit of the ancient Greek, but because they lack it.

The period of the Renascence is commonly called that of the "Revival of Letters," as if the influences then brought to bear upon the mind of Western Europe has been wholly exhausted in the field of literature. I think it is very commonly forgotten that the revival of science, effected by the same agency, although less conspicuous, was not less momentous.

In fact, the few and scattered students of nature of that day picked up the clue to her secrets exactly as it fell from the hands of the Greeks a thousand years before. The foundations of mathematics were so well laid by them, that our children learn their geometry from a book written for the schools of Alexandria two thousand years ago. Modern astronomy is the natural continuation and development of the work of Hipparchus and of Ptolemy; modern physics of that of Democritus and of Archimedes; it was long before modern biological science outgrew the knowledge bequeathed to us by Aristotle, by Theophrastus, and by Galen.

We cannot know all the best thoughts and sayings of the Greeks unless we know what they thought about natural phenomena. We cannot fully apprehend their criticism of life unless we understand the extent to which that criticism was affected by scientific conceptions. We falsely pretend to be the inheritors of their culture, unless we are penetrated, as the best minds among them were, with an unhesitating faith that the free employment of reason, in accordance with scientific method, is the sole method of reaching truth.

Thus I venture to think that the pretensions of our modern Humanists to the possession of the monopoly of culture and to the exclusive inheritance of the spirit of antiquity must be abated, if not abandoned. But I should be very sorry that anything I have said should be taken to imply a desire on my part to depreciate the value of classical education, as it might be and as it sometimes is. The native capacities of mankind vary no less than their opportunities; and while culture is one, the road by which one man may best reach it is widely different from that which is most advantageous to another. Again, while scientific education is yet inchoate and tentative, classical education is thoroughly well organized upon the practical experience of generations of teachers. So that, given ample time for learning and destination for ordinary life, or for a literary career, I do not think that a young Englishman in search of culture can do better than follow the course usually marked out for him, supplementing its deficiencies by his own efforts.

But for those who mean to make science their serious occupation; or who intend to follow the profession of medicine; or who have to enter early upon the business of life; for all these, in my opinion, classical education is a mistake; and it is for this reason that I am glad to see "mere literary education and instruction" shut out from the curriculum of Sir Josiah Mason's College, seeing that its inclusion would probably lead to the introduction of the ordinary smattering of Latin and Greek.

Nevertheless, I am the last person to question the importance of genuine literary education, or to suppose that intellectual culture can be complete without it. An exclusively scientific training will bring about a mental twist as surely as an exclusively literary training. The value of the cargo does not compensate for a ship's being out of trim; and I should be very sorry to think that the Scientific College would turn out none but lop-sided men.

There is no need, however, that such a catastrophe should happen. Instruction in English, French, and German is provided, and thus the three greatest literatures of the modern world are made accessible to the student.

French and German, and especially the latter language, are absolutely indispensable to those who desire full knowledge in any department of science. But even supposing that the knowledge of these languages acquired is not more than sufficient for purely scientific purposes, every Englishman has, in his native tongue, an almost perfect instrument of literary expression; and, in his own literature, models of every kind of literary excellence. If an Englishman cannot get literary culture out of his Bible, his Shakespeare, his Milton, neither, in my belief, will the profoundest study of Homer and Sophocles, Virgil and Horace, give it to him.

Thus, since the constitution of the College makes sufficient provision for literary as well as for scientific education, and since artistic instruction is also contemplated, it seems to me that a fairly complete culture is offered to all who are willing to take advantage of it.

But I am not sure that at this point the "practical" man, scotched but not slain, may ask what all this talk about culture has to do with an Institution, the object of which is defined to be "to promote the prosperity of the manufactures and the industry of the country." He may suggest that what is wanted for this end is not culture, nor even a purely scientific discipline, but simply a knowledge of applied science.

I often wish that this phrase, "applied science," had never been invented. For it suggests that there is a sort of scientific knowledge of direct practical use, which can be studied apart from another sort of scientific knowledge, which is of no practical utility, and which is termed "pure science." But there is no more complete fallacy than this. What people call applied science is nothing but the application of pure science to particular classes of problems. It consists of deductions from those general principles, established by reasoning and observation, which constitute pure science. No one can safely make these deductions until he has a firm grasp of the principles; and he can obtain that grasp only by personal experience of the operations of observation and of reasoning on which they are founded.

Almost all the processes employed in the arts and manufactures fall within the range either of physics or of chemistry. In order to improve them, one must thoroughly understand them; and no one has a chance of really understanding them, unless he has obtained that mastery of principles and that habit of dealing with facts, which is given by long-continued and well-directed purely scientific training in the physical and the chemical laboratory. So that there really is no question as to the necessity of purely scientific discipline, even if the work of the College were limited by the narrowest interpretation of its stated aims.

And, as to the desirableness of a wider culture than that yielded by science alone, it is to be recollected that the improvement of manufacturing processes is only one of the conditions which contribute to the prosperity of industry. Industry is a means and not an end; and mankind work only to get something which they want. What that something is depends partly on their innate, and partly on their acquired, desires.

If the wealth resulting from prosperous industry is to be spent upon the gratification of unworthy desires, if the increasing perfection of manufacturing processes is to be accompanied by an increasing debasement of those who carry them on, I do not see the good of industry and prosperity.

Now it is perfectly true that men's views of what is desirable depend upon their characters; and that the innate proclivities to which we give that name are not touched by any amount of instruction. But it does not follow that even mere intellectual education may not, to an indefinite extent, modify the practical manifestation of the characters of men in their actions, by supplying them with motives unknown to the ignorant. A pleasure-loving character will have pleasure of some sort; but, if you give him the choice, he may prefer pleasures which do not degrade him to those which do. And this choice is offered to every man, who possesses in literary or artistic culture a never-failing source of pleasures, which are neither withered by age, nor staled by custom, nor embittered in the recollection by the pangs of self-reproach.

If the Institution opened to-day fulfills the intention of its founder, the picked intelligences among all classes of the population of this district will pass through it. No child born in Birmingham, henceforward, if he have the capacity to profit by the opportunities offered to him, first in the primary and other schools, and afterward in the Scientific College, need fail to obtain, not merely the instruction, but the culture most appropriate to the conditions of his life.

Within these walls, the future employer and the future artisan may sojourn together for awhile, and carry, through all their lives, the stamp of the influences then brought to bear upon them. Hence, it is not beside the mark to remind you, that the prosperity of industry depends not merely upon the improvement of manufacturing processes, not merely upon the ennobling of the individual character, but upon a third condition, namely, a clear understanding of the conditions of social life on the part of both the capitalist and the operative, and their agreement upon common principles of social action. They must learn that social phenomena are as much the expression of natural laws as any others; that no social arrangements can be permanent unless they harmonize with the requirements of social statics and dynamics; and that, in the nature of things, there is an arbiter whose decisions execute themselves.

But this knowledge is only to be obtained by the application of the methods of investigation adopted in physical researches to the investigation of the phenomena of society. Hence, I confess, I should like to see one addition made to the excellent scheme of education propounded for the College, in the shape of provision for the teaching of Sociology. For though we are all agreed that party politics are to have no place in the instruction of the College; yet in this country, practically governed as it is now by universal suffrage, every man who does his duty must exercise political functions. And, if the evils which are inseparable from the good of political liberty are to be checked, if the perpetual oscillation of nations between anarchy and despotism is to be replaced by the steady march of self-restraining freedom; it will be because men will gradually bring themselves to deal with political, as they now deal with scientific questions; to be as ashamed of undue haste and partisan prejudice in the one case as in the other; and to believe that the machinery of society is at least as delicate as that of a spinning-jenny, and as little likely to be improved by the meddling of those who have not taken the trouble to master the principles of its action.

In conclusion, I am sure that I make myself the mouthpiece of all present in offering to the venerable founder of the Institution, which now commences its beneficent career, our congratulations on the completion of his work; and in expressing the conviction, that the remotest posterity will point to it as a crucial instance of the wisdom which natural piety leads all men to ascribe to their ancestors.

III.

ON ELEMENTARY INSTRUCTION IN PHYSIOLOGY.*

THE chief ground upon which I venture to recommend that the teaching of elementary physiology should form an essential part of any organized course of instruction in matters pertaining to domestic economy, is, that a knowledge of even the elements of this subject supplies those conceptions of the constitution and mode of action of the living body, and of the nature of health and disease, which prepare the mind to receive instruction from sanitary science.

It is, I think, eminently desirable that the hygienist and the physician should find something in the public mind to which they can appeal; some little stock of universally acknowledged truths, which may serve as a foundation for their warnings, and predispose toward an intelligent obedience to their recommendations.

Listening to ordinary talk about health, disease, and death, one is often led to entertain a doubt whether the speakers believe that the course of natural causation runs as smoothly in the human body as elsewhere. Indications are too often obvious of a strong, though perhaps an unavowed and half unconscious, undercurrent of opinion that the phenomena of life are not only widely different, in their superficial characters and in their practical importance, from other natural events, but that they do not follow in that definite order which characterizes the succession of all other occurrences, and the statement of which we call a law of nature.

* Read at the Domestic Economy Congress, Birmingham (1877).

Hence, I think, arises the want of heartiness of belief in the value of knowledge respecting the laws of health and disease, and of the foresight and care to which knowledge is the essential preliminary, which is so often noticeable; and a corresponding laxity and carelessness in practice, the results of which are too frequently lamentable.

It is said that among the many religious sects of Russia, there is one which holds that all disease is brought about by the direct and special interference of the Deity, and which, therefore, looks with repugnance, upon both preventive and curative measures as alike blasphemous interferences with the will of God. Among ourselves, the "Peculiar People" are, I believe, the only persons who hold the like doctrine in its integrity, and carry it out with logical rigor. But many of us are old enough to recollect that the administration of chloroform in assuagement of the pangs of childbirth was, at its introduction, strenuously resisted upon similar grounds.

I am not sure that the feeling, of which the doctrine to which I have referred is the full expression, does not lie at the bottom of the minds of a great many people who yet would vigorously object to give a verbal assent to the doctrine itself. However this may be, the main point is that sufficient knowledge has now been acquired of vital phenomena, to justify the assertion, that the notion, that there is anything exceptional about these phenomena, receives not a particle of support from any known fact. On the contrary, there is a vast and an increasing mass of evidence that birth and death, health and disease, are as much parts of the ordinary stream of events as the rising and setting of the sun, or the changes of the moon; and that the living body is a mechanism, the proper working of which we term health; its disturbance, disease; its stoppage, death.

The activity of this mechanism is dependent upon many and complicated conditions, some of which are hopelessly beyond our control, while others are readily accessible, and are capable of being indefinitely modified by our own actions. The business of the hygienist and of the physician is to know the range of these modifiable conditions, and how to influence them toward the maintenance of health and the prolongation of life; the business of the general public is to give an intelligent assent, and a ready obedience based upon that assent, to the rules laid down for their guidance by such experts. But an intelligent assent is an assent based upon knowledge, and the knowledge which is here in question means an acquaintance with the elements of physiology.

It is not difficult to acquire such knowledge. What is true, to a certain extent, of all the physical sciences, is eminently characteristic of physiology—the difficulty of the subject begins beyond the stage of elementary knowledge, and increases with every stage of progress. While the most highly trained and the best furnished intellect may find all its resources insufficient, when it strives to reach the heights and penetrate into the depths of the problems of physiology, the elementary and fundamental truths can be made clear to a child.

No one can have any difficulty in comprehending the mechanism of circulation or respiration; or the general mode of operation of the organ of vision; though the unraveling of all the minutiæ of these processes, may, for the present, baffle the conjoined attacks of the most accomplished physicists, chemists, and mathematicians. To know the anatomy of the human body, with even an approximation to thoroughness, is the work of a life; but as much as is needed for a sound comprehension of elementary physiological truths, may be learned in a week.

A knowledge of the elements of physiology is not only easy of acquirement, but it may be made a real and practical acquaintance with the facts, as far as it goes. The subject of study is always at hand, in oneself. The principal constituents of the skeleton, and the changes of form of contracting muscles, may be felt through one's own skin. The beating of one's heart, and its connection with the pulse, may be noted; the influence of the valves of one's own veins may be shown; the movements of respiration may be observed; while the wonderful phenomena of sensation afford an endless field for curious and interesting self-study. The prick of a needle will yield, in a drop of one's own blood, material for microscopic observation of phenomena which lie at the foundation of all biological conceptions; and a cold, with its concomitant coughing and sneezing, may prove the sweet uses of adversity by helping one to a clear conception of what is meant by "reflex action."

Of course there is a limit to this physiological self-examination. But there is so close a solidarity between ourselves and our poor relations of the animal world, that our inaccessible inward parts may be supplemented by theirs. A comparative anatomist knows that a sheep's heart and lungs, or eye, must not be confounded with those of a man; but, so far as the comprehension of the elementary facts of the physiology of circulation, of respiration, and of vision goes, the one furnishes the needful anatomical data as well as the other.

Thus, it is quite possible to give instruction in elementary physiology in such a manner as, not only to confer knowledge, which, for the reason I have mentioned, is useful in itself; but to serve the purposes of a training in accurate observation, and in the methods of reasoning of physical science. But that is an advantage which I mention only incidentally, as the present Conference does not deal with education in the ordinary sense of word.

It will not be suspected that I wish to make physiologists of all the world. It would be as reasonable to accuse an advocate of the "three R's" of a desire to make an orator, an author, and a mathematician of everybody. A stumbling reader, a pot-hook writer, and an arithmetician who has not got beyond the rule of three, is not a person of brilliant acquirements; but the difference between such a member of society and one who can neither read, write, nor cipher is almost inexpressible; and no one now-a-days doubts the value of instruction, even if it goes no farther.

The saying that a little knowledge is a dangerous thing is, to my mind, a very dangerous adage. If knowledge is real and genuine, I do not believe that it is other than a very valuable possession, however infinitesimal its quantity may be. Indeed, if a little knowledge is dangerous, where is the man who has so much as to be out of danger?

If William Harvey's life-long labors had revealed to him a tenth part of that which may be made sound and real knowledge to our boys and girls, he would not only have been what he was, the greatest physiologist of his age, but he would have loomed upon the seventeenth century as a sort of intellectual portent. Our "little knowledge" would have been to him a great, astounding, unlooked-for vision of scientific truth.

I really see no harm which can come of giving our children a little knowledge of physiology. But then, as I have said, the instruction must be real, based upon observation, eked out by good explanatory diagrams and models, and conveyed by a teacher whose own knowledge has been acquired by a study of the facts; and not the mere catechismal parrot-work which too often usurps the place of elementary teaching.

It is, I hope, unnecessary for me to give a formal contradiction to the silly fiction, which is assiduously circulated by fanatics who not only ought to know, but do know, that their assertions are untrue, that I have advocated the introduction of that experimental discipline which is absolutely indispensable to the professed physiologist, into elementary teaching.

But while I should object to any experimentation which can justly be called painful, for the purpose of elementary instruction; and, while, as a member of a late Royal Commission, I gladly did my best to prevent the infliction of needless pain, for any purpose; I think it is my duty to take this opportunity of expressing my regret at a condition of the law which permits a boy to troll for pike, or set lines with live frog bait, for idle amusement; and, at the same time, lays the teacher of that boy open to the penalty of fine and imprisonment, if he uses the same animal for the purpose of exhibiting one of the most beautiful and instructive of physiological spectacles, the circulation in the web of the foot. No one could undertake to affirm that a frog is not inconvenienced by being wrapped up in a wet rag, and having his toes tied out; and it cannot be denied that inconvenience is a sort of pain. But you must not inflict the least pain on a vertebrated animal for scientific purposes (though you may do a good deal in that way for gain or for sport) without due license of the Secretary of State for the Home Department, granted under the authority of the Vivisection Act.

So it comes about, that, in this present year of grace 1877, two persons may be charged with cruelty to animals. One has impaled a frog, and suffered the creature to writhe about in that condition for hours; the other has pained the animal no more than one of us would be pained by tying strings round his fingers and keeping him in the position of a hydropathic patient. The first offender says, "I did it because I find fishing very amusing," and the magistrate bids him depart in peace; nay, probably wishes him good sport. The second pleads, "I wanted to impress a scientific truth, with a distinctness attainable in no other way, on the minds of my scholars," and the magistrate fines him five pounds.

I cannot but think that this is an anomalous and not wholly creditable state of things.

IV.

ON THE BORDER TERRITORY BETWEEN THE ANIMAL AND THE VEGETABLE KINGDOMS.*

IN the whole history of science there is nothing more remarkable than the rapidity of the growth of biological knowledge within the last half-century, and the extent of the modification which has thereby been effected in some of the fundamental conceptions of the naturalist.

In the second edition of the "Règne Animal," published in 1828, Cuvier devotes a special section to the "Division of Organized Beings into Animals and Vegetables," in which the question is treated with that comprehensiveness of knowledge and clear critical judgment which characterize his writings, and justify us in regarding them as representative expressions of the most extensive, if not the profoundest, knowledge of his time. He tells us that living beings have been subdivided from the earliest times into *animated beings*, which possess sense and motion, and *inanimated beings*, which are devoid of these functions, and simply vegetate.

Although the roots of plants direct themselves toward moisture, and their leaves toward air and light,—although the parts of some plants exhibit oscillating movements without any perceptible cause, and the leaves of others retract when touched,—yet none of these movements justify the ascription to plants of perception or of will. From the mobility of animals, Cuvier, with his characteristic partiality for teleological reasoning, deduces the necessity of the existence in them of an alimentary cavity, or reservoir of food, whence their nutrition may be drawn by the vessels which are a sort of internal roots; and, in the presence of this alimentary cavity, he naturally sees the primary and the most important distinction between animals and plants.

Following out his teleological argument, Cuvier remarks that the organization of this cavity and its appurtenances must needs vary according to the nature

* Lecture at the Royal Institution, London (1876).

of the aliment, and the operations which it has to undergo, before it can be converted into substances fitted for absorption; while the atmosphere and the earth supply plants with juices ready prepared, and which can be absorbed immediately. As the animal body required to be independent of heat and of the atmosphere, there were no means by which the motion of its fluids could be produced by internal causes. Hence arose the second great distinctive character of animals, or the circulatory system, which is less important than the digestive, since it was unnecessary, and therefore is absent, in the more simple animals.

Animals further needed muscles for locomotion and nerves for sensibility. Hence, says Cuvier, it was necessary that the chemical composition of the animal body should be more complicated than that of the plant; and it is so, inasmuch as an additional substance, nitrogen, enters into it as an essential element; while, in plants, nitrogen is only accidentally joined with the three other fundamental constituents of organic beings—carbon, hydrogen, and oxygen. Indeed, he afterward affirms that nitrogen is peculiar to animals; and herein he places the third distinction between the animal and the plant. The soil and the atmosphere supply plants with water, composed of hydrogen and oxygen; air, consisting of nitrogen and oxygen; and carbonic acid, containing carbon and oxygen. They retain the hydrogen and the carbon, exhale the superfluous oxygen, and absorb little or no nitrogen. The essential character of vegetable life is the exhalation of oxygen, which is effected through the agency of light. Animals, on the contrary, derive their nourishment either directly or indirectly from plants. They get rid of the superfluous hydrogen and carbon, and accumulate nitrogen. The relations of plants and animals to the atmosphere are therefore inverse. The plant withdraws water and carbonic acid from the atmosphere, the animal contributes both to it. Respiration—that is, the absorption of oxygen and the exhalation of carbonic acid—is the specially animal function of animals, and constitutes their fourth distinctive character.

Thus wrote Cuvier in 1828. But, in the fourth and fifth decades of this century, the greatest and most rapid revolution which biological science has ever undergone was effected by the application of the modern microscope to the investigation of organic structure; by the introduction of exact and easily manageable methods of conducting the chemical analysis of organic compounds; and finally, by the employment of instruments of precision for the measurement of the physical forces which are at work in the living economy.

That the semi-fluid contents (which we now term protoplasm) of the cells of certain plants, such as the *Charæ*, are in constant and regular motion, was made out by Bonaventura Corti a century ago; but the fact, important as it was, fell into oblivion, and had to be re-discovered by Treviranus in 1807. Robert Brown noted the more complex motions of the protoplasm in the cells of *Trádescantia* in 1831; and now such movements of the living substance of plants are well known to be some of the most widely-prevalent phenomena of vegetable life.

Agardh, and other of the botanists of Cuvier's generation, who occupied themselves with the lower plants, had observed that, under particular circumstances, the contents of the cells of certain water-weeds were set free, and moved about with considerable velocity, and with all the appearances of spontaneity, as locomotive bodies, which, from their similarity to animals of simple organization, were called "zoospores." Even as late as 1845, however, a botanist of Schleiden's eminence dealt very sceptically with these statements; and his scepticism was the more justified, since Ehrenberg, in his elaborate and comprehensive work on the *Infusoria*, had declared the greater number of what are now recognized as locomotive plants to be animals.

At the present day, innumerable plants and free plant cells are known to pass the whole or part of their lives in an actively locomotive condition, in no wise distinguishable from that of one of the simpler animals; and, while in this condition, their movements are, to all appearance, as spontaneous—as much the product of volition—as those of such animals.

Hence the teleological argument for Cuvier's first diagnostic character—the presence in animals of an alimentary cavity, or internal pocket, in which they can carry about their nutriment—has broken down, so far, at least, as his mode of stating it goes. And, with the advance of microscopic anatomy, the universality of the fact itself among animals has ceased to be predicable. Many animals of even complex structure, which live parasitically within others, are wholly devoid of an alimentary cavity. Their food is provided for them, not only ready cooked, but ready digested, and the alimentary canal, become superfluous, has disappeared. Again, the males of most Rotifers have no digestive apparatus; as a German naturalist has remarked, they devote themselves entirely to the "Minnedienst," and are to be reckoned among the few realizations of the Byronic ideal of a lover. Finally, amidst the lowest forms of animal life, the speck of gelatinous protoplasm, which constitutes the whole body, has no permanent digestive cavity or mouth, but takes in its food anywhere; and digests, so to speak, all over its body.

But although Cuvier's leading diagnosis of the animal from the plant will not stand a strict test, it remains one of the most constant of the distinctive characters of animals. And, if we substitute for the possession of an alimentary cavity, the power of taking solid nutriment into the body and their digesting it, the definition so changed will cover all animals, except certain parasites, and the few and exceptional cases of non-parasitic animals which do not feed at all. On the other hand, the definition thus amended will exclude all ordinary vegetable organisms.

Cuvier himself practically gives up his second distinctive mark when he admits that it is wanting in the simpler animals.

The third distinction is based on a completely erroneous conception of the chemical differences and resemblances between the constituents of animal and vegetable organisms, for which Cuvier is not responsible, as it was current among contemporary chemists. It is now established that nitrogen is as essential a constituent of vegetable as of animal living matter; and that the latter is, chemically speaking, just as complicated as the former. Starchy substances, cellulose and sugar, once supposed to be exclusively confined to plants, are now known to be regular and normal products of animals. Amylaceous and saccharine substances are largely manufactured, even by the highest animals; cellulose is widespread as a constituent of the skeletons of the lower animals; and it is probable that amyloid substances are universally present in the animal organism, though not in the precise form of starch.

Moreover, although it remains true that there is an inverse relation between the green plant in sunshine and the animal, in so far as, under these circumstances, the green plant decomposes carbonic acid and exhales oxygen, while the animal absorbs oxygen and exhales carbonic acid; yet, the exact investigations of the modern chemical investigators of the physiological processes of plants have clearly demonstrated the fallacy of attempting to draw any general distinction between animals and vegetables on this ground. In fact, the difference vanishes with the sunshine, even in the case of the green plant; which, in the dark, absorbs oxygen and gives out carbonic acid like any animal.* On the other hand, those plants, such as the fungi, which contain no chlorophyll and are not green, are always, so far as respiration is concerned, in the exact position of animals. They absorb oxygen and give out carbonic acid.

Thus, by the progress of knowledge, Cuvier's fourth distinction between the animal and the plant has been as completely invalidated as the third and second; and even the first can be retained only in a modified form and subject to exceptions.

But has the advance of biology simply tended to break down old distinctions, without establishing new ones?

With a qualification, to be considered presently, the answer to this question is undoubtedly in the affirmative. The famous researches of Schwann and Schleiden in 1837 and the following years, founded the modern science of histology, or that branch of anatomy which deals with the ultimate visible structure of organisms, as revealed by the microscope; and, from that day to this, the rapid improvement of methods of investigation, and the energy of a host of accurate observers, have given greater and greater breadth and firmness to Schwann's great generalization, that a fundamental unity of structure obtains in animals and plants; and that, however diverse may be the fabrics, or *tissues*, of which their bodies are composed, all these varied structures result from the metamorphosis of morphological units (termed *cells*, in a more general sense than that in which the word "cells" was at first employed), which are not only similar in animals and in plants respectively, but present a close resemblance, when those of animals and those of plants are compared together.

The contractility which is the fundamental condition of locomotion, has not

* There is every reason to believe that living plants, like living animals, always respire, and, in respiring, absorb oxygen and give off carbonic acid; but, that in green plants exposed to daylight or to the electric light, the quantity of oxygen evolved in consequence of the decomposition of carbonic acid by a special apparatus which green plants possess exceeds that absorbed in the concurrent respiratory process.

only been discovered to exist far more widely among plants than was formerly imagined; but, in plants, the act of contraction has been found to be accompanied, as Dr. Burdon Sanderson's interesting investigations have shown, by a disturbance of the electrical state of the contractile substance, comparable to that which was found by Du Bois Reymond to be a concomitant of the activity of ordinary muscle in animals.

Again, I know of no test by which the reaction of the leaves of the Sundew and of other plants to stimuli, so fully and carefully studied by Mr. Darwin, can be distinguished from those acts of contraction following upon stimuli, which are called "reflex" in animals.

On each lobe of the bilobed leaf of Venus's fly trap (*Dionæa muscipula*) are three delicate filaments which stand out at right angle from the surface of the leaf. Touch one of them with the end of a fine human hair and the lobes of the leaf instantly close together * in virtue of an act of contraction of part of their substance, just as the body of a snail contracts into its shell when one of its "horns" is irritated.

The reflex action of the snail is the result of the presence of a nervous system in the animal. A molecular change takes place in the nerve of the tentacle, is propagated to the muscles by which the body is retracted, and causing them to contract, the act of retraction is brought about. Of course the similarity of the acts does not necessarily involve the conclusion that the mechanism by which they are effected is the same; but it suggests a suspicion of their identity which needs careful testing.

The results of recent inquiries into the structure of the nervous system of animals converge toward the conclusion that the nerve fibers, which we have hitherto regarded as ultimate elements of nervous tissue, are not such, but are simply the visible aggregations of vastly more attenuated filaments, the diameter of which dwindles down to the limits of our present microscopic vision, greatly as these have been extended by modern improvements of the microscope; and that a nerve is, in its essence, nothing but a linear tract of specially modified protoplasm between two points of an organism—one of which is able to affect the other by means of the communication so established. Hence, it is conceivable that even the simplest living being may possess a nervous system. And the question whether plants are provided with a nervous system or not, thus acquires a new aspect, and presents the histologist and physiologist with a problem of extreme difficulty, which must be attacked from a new point of view and by the aid of methods which have yet to be invented.

* Darwin, "Insectivorous Plants," p. 289.

Thus it must be admitted that plants may be contractile and locomotive; that, while locomotive, their movements may have as much appearance of spontaneity as those of the lowest animals; and that many exhibit actions, comparable to those which are brought about by the agency of a nervous system in animals. And it must be allowed to be possible that further research may reveal the existence of something comparable to a nervous system in plants. So that I know not where we can hope to find any absolute distinction between animals and plants, unless we return to their mode of nutrition, and inquire whether certain differences of a more occult character than those imagined to exist by Cuvier, and which hold good for the vast majority of animals and plants, are of universal application.

A bean may be supplied with water in which salts of ammonia and certain other mineral salts are dissolved in due proportion; with atmospheric air containing its ordinary minute dose of carbonic acid; and with nothing else but sunlight and heat. Under these circumstances, unnatural as they are, with proper management, the bean will thrust forth its radicle and its plumule; the former will grow down into roots, the latter grow up into the stem and leaves, of a vigorous bean plant; and this plant will, in due time, flower and produce its crop of beans, just as if it were grown in the garden or in the field.

The weight of the nitrogenous protein compounds, of the oily, starchy, saccharine and woody substances contained in the full-grown plant and its seeds, will be vastly greater than the weight of the same substances contained in the bean from which it sprang. But nothing has been supplied to the bean save water, carbonic acid, ammonia, potash, lime, iron, and the like, in combination with phosphoric, sulphuric, and other acids. Neither protein, nor fat, nor starch, nor sugar, nor any substance in the slightest degree resembling them, has formed part of the food of the bean. But the weights of the carbon, hydrogen, oxygen, nitrogen, phosphorus, sulphur, and other elementary bodies contained in the bean-plant, and in the seeds which it produces, are exactly equivalent to the weights of the same elements which have disappeared from the materials supplied to the bean during its growth. Whence it follows that the bean has taken in only the raw materials of its fabric, and has manufactured them into bean stuffs.

The bean has been able to perform this great chemical feat by the help of its green coloring matter, or chlorophyll; for it is only the green parts of the plant which, under the influence of sunlight, have the marvelous power of decomposing carbonic acid, setting free the oxygen and laying hold of the carbon which it contains. In fact, the bean obtains two of the absolutely indispensable elements of its substance from two distinct sources: the watery solution, in which its roots are plunged, contains nitrogen but no carbon; the air, to which the leaves are exposed, contains carbon, but its nitrogen is in the state of a free gas, in which condition the bean can make no use of it;* and the chlorophyll † is the apparatus by which the carbon is extracted from the atmospheric carbonic acid—the leaves being the chief laboratories in which this operation is effected.

The great majority of conspicuous plants are, as everybody knows, green; and this arises from the abundance of their chlorophyll. The few which contain no chlorophyll and are colorless, are unable to extract the carbon which they require from atmospheric carbonic acid, and lead a parasitic existence upon other plants; but it by no means follows, often as the statement has been repeated, that the manufacturing power of plants depends on their chlorophyll, and its interaction with the rays of the sun. On the contrary, it is easily demonstrated, as Pasteur first proved, that the lowest fungi, devoid of chlorophyll, or of any substitute for it, as they are, nevertheless possess the characteristic manufacturing powers of plants in a very high degree. Only it is necessary that they should be supplied with a different kind of raw material; as they cannot extract carbon from carbonic acid, they must be furnished with something else that contains carbon. Tartaric acid is such a substance; and if a single spore of the commonest and most troublesome of molds—*Penicillium*—be sown in a saucerful of water, in which tartrate of ammonia, with a small percentage of phosphates and sulphates is contained, and kept warm whether in the dark or exposed to light, it will, in a short time, give rise to a thick crust of mold, which contains many million times the weight of the original spore, in protein compounds and cellulose. Thus we have a very wide basis of fact for the generalization that plants are essentially characterized by their manufacturing capacity—by their power of working up mere mineral matters into complex organic compounds.

Contrariwise, there is a no less wide foundation for the generalization that animals, as Cuvier puts it, depend directly or indirectly upon plants for the materials of their bodies; that is, either they are herbivorous, or they eat other animals which are herbivorous.

But for what constituents of their bodies are animals thus dependent upon plants? Certainly not for their horny matter; nor for chondrin, the proximate chemical element of cartilage; nor for gelatine; nor for syntonin, the constituent of muscle; nor for their nervous or biliary substances; nor for their amyloid matters; nor, necessarily, for their fats.

It can be experimentally demonstrated that animals can make these for themselves. But that which they cannot make, but must, in all known cases, obtain directly or indirectly from plants, is the peculiar nitrogenous matter, protein. Thus the plant is the ideal *prolétaire* of the living world, the worker who produces; the animal, the ideal aristocrat, who mostly occupies himself in consuming, after the manner of that noble representative of the line of Zähdarm, whose epitaph is written in *Sartor Resartus*.

Here is our last hope of finding a sharp line of demarkation between plants and animals; for, as I have already hinted, there is a border territory between the two kingdoms, a sort of no-man's-land, the inhabitants of which certainly cannot be discriminated and brought to their proper allegiances in any other way.

Some months ago, Professor Tyndall asked me to examine a drop of infusion of hay, placed under an excellent and powerful microscope, and to tell him what I thought some organisms visible in it were. I looked and observed, in the first place, multitudes of *Bacteria* moving about with their ordinary intermittent

* I purposely assume that the air with which the bean is supplied in the case stated contains no ammoniacal salts.

† The recent researches of Pringsheim have raised a host of questions as to the exact share taken by chlorophyll in the chemical operations which are effected by the green parts of plants. It may be that the chlorophyll is only a constant concomitant of the actual deoxidizing apparatus.

spasmodic wriggles. As to the vegetable nature of these there is now no doubt. Not only does the close resemblance of the *Bacteria* to unquestionable plants, such as the *Oscillatoriæ*, and lower forms of *Fungi*, justify this conclusion, but the manufacturing test settles the question at once. It is only needful to add a minute drop of fluid containing *Bacteria*, to water in which tartrate, phosphate, and sulphate of ammonia are dissolved; and, in a very short space of time, the clear fluid becomes milky by reason of their prodigious multiplication, which, of course, implies the manufacture of living Bacterium-stuff out of these merely saline matters.

But other active organisms, very much larger than the *Bacteria*, attaining in fact the comparatively gigantic dimensions of one-three thousandths of an inch or more, incessantly crossed the field of view. Each of these had a body shaped like a pear, the small end being slightly incurved and produced into a long curved filament, or *cilium*, of extreme tenuity. Behind this, from the concave side of the incurvation, proceeded another long cilium, so delicate as to be discernible only by the use of the highest powers and careful management of the light. In the center of the pear-shaped body a clear round space could occasionally be discerned, but not always; and careful watching showed that this clear vacuity appeared gradually, and then shut up and disappeared suddenly, at regular intervals. Such a structure is of common occurrence among the lowest plants and animals, and is known as a *contractile vacuole*.

The little creature thus described sometimes propelled itself with great activity, with a curious rolling motion, by the lashing of the front cilium, while the second cilium trailed behind; sometimes it anchored itself by the hinder cilium and was spun round by the working of the other, its motions resembling those of an anchor buoy in a heavy sea. Sometimes, when two were in full career toward one another, each would appear dexterously to get out of the other's way; sometimes a crowd would assemble and jostle one another, with as much semblance of individual effort as a spectator on the Grands Mulets might observe with a telescope among the specks representing men in the valley of Chamounix.

The spectacle, though always surprising, was not new to me. So my reply to the question put to me was, that these organisms were what biologists call *Monads*, and though they might be animals, it was also possible that they might, like the *Bacteria*, be plants. My friend received my verdict with an expression which showed a sad want of respect for authority. He would as soon believe that a sheep was a plant. Naturally piqued by this want of faith, I have thought a good deal over the matter; and as I still rest in the lame conclusion I originally expressed, and must even now confess that I cannot certainly say whether this creature is an animal or a plant, I think it may be well to state the grounds of my hesitation at length. But in the first place, in order that I may conveniently distinguish this "Monad" from the multitude of other things which go by the same designation, I must give it a name of its own. I think (though for reasons which need not be stated at present, I am not quite sure) that it is identical with the species *Monas lens*, as defined by the eminent French microscopist Dujardin, though his magnifying power was probably insufficient to enable him to see that it is curiously like a much larger form of monad which he has named *Heteromita*, I shall, therefore, call it not *Monas*, but *Heteromita lens*.

I have been unable to devote to my *Heteromita* the prolonged study needful to work out its whole history, which would involve weeks, or it may be months, of unremitting attention. But I the less regret this circumstance, as some remarkable observations recently published by Messrs. Dallinger and Drysdale * on certain Monads, relate, in part, to a form so similar to my *Heteromita lens*, that the history of the one may be used to illustrate that of the other. These most patient and painstaking observers, who employed the highest attainable powers of the microscope and, relieving one another, kept watch day and night over the same individual monads, have been enabled to trace out the whole history of their *Heteromita*; which they found in infusions of the heads of fishes of the Cod tribe.

Of the four monads described and figured by these investigators, one, as I have said, very closely resembles *Heteromita lens* in every particular, except that it has a separately distinguishable central particle or "nucleus," which is not certainly to be made out in *Heteromita lens*; and that nothing is said by Messrs. Dallinger and Drysdale of the existence of a con-

* "Researches in the Life-history of a Cercomonad: a Lesson in Biogenesis;" and "Further Researches in the Life-history of the Monads."—*Monthly Microscopical Journal*. 1873.

tractile vacuole in this monad, though they describe it in another.

Their *Heteromita*, however, multiplied rapidly by fission. Sometimes a transverse constriction appeared, the hinder half developed a new cilium, and the hinder cilium gradually split from its base to its free end, until it was divided into two; a process which, considering the fact that this fine filament cannot be much more than one-one hundred thousandths of an inch in diameter, is wonderful enough. The constriction of the body extended inward until the two portions were united by a narrow isthmus; finally, they separated and each swam away by itself, a complete *Heteromita*, provided with its two cilia. Sometimes the constriction took a longitudinal direction, with the same ultimate result. In each case the process occupied not more than six or seven minutes. At this rate, a single *Heteromita* would give rise to a thousand like itself in the course of an hour, to about a million in two hours, and to a number greater than the generally assumed number of human beings now living in the world in three hours; or, if we give each *Heteromita* an hour's enjoyment of individual existence, the same result will be obtained in about a day. The apparent suddenness of the appearance of multitudes of such organisms as these, in any nutritive fluid to which one obtains access, is thus easily explained.

During these processes of multiplication by fission, the *Heteromita* remains active; but sometimes another mode of fission occurs. The body becomes rounded and quiescent, or nearly so; and, while in this resting state, divides into two portions, each of which is rapidly converted into an active *Heteromita*.

A still more remarkable phenomenon is that kind of multiplication which is preceded by the union of two monads, by a process which is termed *conjugation*. Two active *Heteromitæ* become applied to one another, and then slowly and gradually coalesce into one body. The two nuclei run into one; and the mass resulting from the conjugation of the two *Heteromitæ*, thus fused together, has a triangular form. The two pairs of cilia are to be seen, for some time, at two of the angles, which answer to the small ends of the conjoined monads; but they ultimately vanish, and the twin organism, in which all visible traces of organization have disappeared, falls into a state of rest. Sudden wave-like movements of its substance next occur; and, in a short time, the apices of the triangular mass burst, and give exit to a dense yellowish, glairy fluid, filled with minute granules. This process, which, it will be observed, involves the actual confluence and mixture of the substance of two distinct organisms, is effected in the space of about two hours.

The authors whom I quote say that they "cannot express" the excessive minuteness of the granules in question, and they estimate their diameter at less than one-two hundred thousandths of an inch. Under the highest powers of the microscope at present applicable such specks are hardly discernible. Nevertheless, particles of this size are massive when compared to physical molecules; whence there is no reason to doubt that each, small as it is, may have a molecular structure sufficiently complex to give rise to the phenomena of life. And, as a matter of fact, by patient watching of the place at which these infinitesimal living particles were discharged, our observers assured themselves of their growth and development into new monads. These, in about four hours from their being set free, had attained a sixth of the length of the parent, with the characteristic cilia, though at first they were quite motionless; and, in four hours more, they had attained the dimensions and exhibited all the activity of the adult. These inconceivably minute particles are therefore the germs of the *Heteromita*; and from the dimensions of these germs it is easily shown that the body formed by conjugation may, at a low estimate, have given exit to thirty thousand of them; a result of a matrimonial process whereby the contracting parties, without a metaphor, "become one flesh," enough to make a Malthusian despair of the future of the Universe.

I am not aware that the investigators from whom I have borrowed this history have endeavored to ascertain whether their monads take solid nutriment or not; so that though they help us very much to fill up the blanks in the history of my *Heteromita*, their observations throw no light on the problem we are trying to solve—Is it an animal or is it a plant?

Undoubtedly it is possible to bring forward very strong arguments in favor of regarding *Heteromita* as a plant.

For example, there is a Fungus, an obscure and almost microscopic mold, termed *Peronospora infestans*. Like many other Fungi, the *Peronosporæ* are parasitic upon other plants; and this particular *Peronospora* happens to have attained much notoriety and political importance, in a way not without a parallel in the career of notorious politicians, namely, by reason of the frightful mischief it has done to mankind. For it is this *Fungus* which is the cause of the potato disease; and, therefore, *Peronospora infestans* (doubtless of exclusively Saxon origin, though not accurately known to be so) brought about the Irish famine. The plants afflicted with the malady are found to be infested by a mold, consisting of fine tubular filaments, termed *hyphæ*, which burrow through the substance of the potato plant, and appropriate to themselves the substance of their host; while, at the same time, directly or indirectly, they set up chemical changes by which even its woody framework becomes blackened, sodden, and withered.

In structure, however, the *Peronospora* in as much a mold as the common *Penicillium;* and just as the *Penicillium* multiplies by the breaking up of its hyphæ into separate rounded bodies, the spores; so, in the *Peronospora*, certain of the hyphæ grow out into the air through the interstices of the superficial cells of the potato plant, and develop spores. Each of these hyphæ usually gives off several branches. The ends of the branches dilate and become closed sacs, which eventually drop off as spores. The spores falling on some part of the same potato plant, or carried by the wind to another, may at once germinate, throwing out tubular prolongations which become hyphæ, and burrow into the substance of the plant attacked. But, more commonly, the contents of the spore divide into six or eight separate portions. The coat of the spore gives way, and each portion then emerges as an independent organism, which has the shape of a bean, rather narrower at one end than the other, convex on one side, and depressed or concave on the opposite. From the depression, two long and delicate cilia proceed, one shorter than the other, and directed forward. Close to the origin of these cilia, in the substance of the body, is a regularly pulsating, contractile vacuole. The shorter cilium vibrates actively, and effects the locomotion of the organism, while the other trails behind; the whole body rolling on its axis with its pointed end forward.

The eminent botanist, De Bary, who was not thinking of our problem, tells us, in describing the movements of these "Zoospores," that, as they swim about, "Foreign bodies are carefully avoided, and the whole movement has a deceptive likeness to the voluntary changes of place which are observed in microscopic animals."

After swarming about in this way in the moisture on the surface of a leaf or stem (which, film though it may be, is an ocean to such a fish) for half an hour, more or less, the movement of the zoospore becomes slower, and is limited to a slow turning upon its axis, without change of place. It then becomes quite quiet, the cilia disappear, it assumes a spherical form, and surrounds itself with a distinct, though delicate, membranous coat. A protuberance then grows out from one side of the sphere, and rapidly increasing in length, assumes the character of a hypha. The latter penetrates into the substance of the potato plant, either by entering a stomate, or by boring through the wall of an epidermic cell and ramifies, as a mycelium, in the substance of the plant, destroying the tissues with which it comes in contact. As these processes of multiplication take place very rapidly, millions of spores are soon set free from a single infested plant; and, from their minuteness, they are readily transported by the gentlest breeze. Since, again, the zoospores set free from each spore, in virtue of their powers of locomotion, swiftly disperse themselves over the surface, it is no wonder that the infection, once started, soon spreads from field to field, and extends its ravages over a whole country.

However, it does not enter into my present plan to treat of the potato disease, instructively as its history bears upon that of other epidemics; and I have selected the case of the *Peronospora* simply because it affords an example of an organism, which, in one stage of its existence, is truly a "Monad," indistinguishable by any important character from our *Heteromita*, and extraordinarily like it in some respects. And yet this "Monad" can be traced, step by step, through the series of metamorphoses which I have described, until it assumes the features of an organism, which is as much a plant as is an oak or an elm.

Moreover, it would be possible to pursue the analogy farther. Under certain circumstances, a process of conjugation takes place in the *Peronospora*. Two separate portions of its protoplasm become fused together, surround themselves with a thick coat, and give rise to a sort of vegetable egg called an *oospore.* After a period of rest, the contents of the oospore break up into a number of zoospores like those already described, each of which, after a period of activity, germinates in the ordinary way. This process obviously corresponds with the conjugation and subsequent setting free of germs in the *Heteromita*.

But it may be said that the *Peronospora* is, after all, a questionable sort of plant; that it seems to be wanting in the manufacturing power, selected as the main distinctive character of vegetable life; or, at any rate, that there is no proof that it does not get its protein matter ready made from the potato plant.

Let us, therefore, take a case which is not open to these objections.

There are some small plants known to botanists as members of the genus *Coleochæte*, which, without being truly parasitic, grow upon certain water-weeds, as lichens grow upon trees. The little plant has the form of an elegant green star, the branching arms of which are divided into cells. Its greenness is due to its chlorophyll, and it undoubtedly has the manufacturing power in full degree, decomposing carbonic acid and setting oxygen free, under the influence of sunlight. But the protoplasmic contents of some of the cells of which the plant is made up occasionally divide, by a method similar to that which effects the division of the contents of the *Peronospora* spore; and the severed portions are then set free as active monad-like zoospores. Each is oval and is provided at one extremity with two long active cilia. Propelled by these, it swims about for a longer or shorter time, but at length comes to a state of rest and gradually grows into a *Coleochæte*. Moreover, as in the *Peronospora*, conjugation may take place and result in an oospore; the contents of which divide and are set free as monadiform germs.

If the whole history of the zoospores of *Peronospora* and of *Coleochæte* were unknown, they would undoubtedly be classed among "Monads" with the same right as *Heteromita*; why then may not *Heteromita* be a plant, even though the cycle of forms through which it passes shows no terms quite so complex as those which occur in *Peronospora* and *Coleochæte*? And, in fact, there are some green organisms, in every respect characteristically plants, such as *Chlamydomonas*, and the common *Volvox*, or so-called "Globe animalcule," which run through a cycle of forms of just the same simple character as those of *Heteromita*.

The name of *Chlamydomonas* is applied to certain microscopic green bodies, each of which consists of a protoplasmic central substance invested by a structureless sac. The latter contains cellulose, as in ordinary plants; and the chlorophyll which gives the green color enables the *Chlamydomonas* to decompose carbonic acid and fix carbon as they do. Two long cilia protrude through the cell-wall, and effect the rapid locomotion of this "monad," which, in all respects except its mobility, is characteristically a plant. Under ordinary circumstances, the *Chlamydomonas* multiplies by simple fission, each splitting into two or into four parts, which separate and become independent organisms. Sometimes, however, the *Chlamydomonas* divides into eight parts, each of which is provided with four instead of two cilia. These "zoospores" conjugate in pairs, and give rise to quiescent bodies, which multiply by division, and eventually pass into the active state.

Thus, so far as outward form and the general character of the cycle of modifications, through which the organism passes in the course of its life, are concerned, the resemblance between *Chlamydomonas* and *Heteromita* is of the closest description. And on the face of the matter there is no ground for refusing to admit that *Heteromita* may be related to *Chlamydomonas*, as the colorless fungus is to the green alga. *Volvox* may be compared to a hollow sphere, the wall of which is made up of coherent Chlamydomonads; and which progresses with a rotating motion effected by the paddling of the multitudinous pairs of cilia which project from its surface. Each *Volvox*-monad, moreover, possesses a red pigment spot, like the simplest form of eye known among animals. The methods of fissive multiplication and of conjugation observed in the monads of this locomotive globe are essentially similar to those observed in *Chlamydomonas*; and, though a hard battle has been fought over it, *Volvox* is now finally surrendered to the Botanists.

Thus there is really no reason why *Heteromita* may not be a plant; and this conclusion would be very satisfactory, if it were not equally easy to show that there is really no reason why it should not be an animal. For there are numerous organisms presenting the closest resemblance to *Heteromita*, and, like it, grouped under the general name of "Monads," which, nevertheless, can be observed to take in solid nutriment, and which, therefore, have a virtual, if not an actual, mouth and digestive cavity, and thus come under Cuvier's definition of an animal. Numerous forms of such animals have been described by Ehrenberg, Dujardin, H. James Clark, and other writers on the *Infusoria*. Indeed, in another infusion of hay in which my *Heteromita lens* occurred, there were innumerable infusorial animalcules belonging to the well-known species *Colpoda cucullus*.*

Full-sized specimens of this animalcule attain a length of between one-three hundredths or one-four hundreths of an inch, so that it may have ten times the length and a thousand times the mass of a *Heteromita*. In shape, it is not altogether unlike *Heteromita*. The small end, however, is not produced into one long cilium, but the general surface of the body is covered with small actively vibrating ciliary organs, which are only longest at the small end. At the point which answers to that from which the two cilia arise in *Heteromita*, there is a conical depression, the mouth; and, in young specimens, a tapering filament, which reminds one of the posterior cilium of *Heteromita*, projects from this region.

The body consists of a soft granular protoplasmic substance, the middle of which is occupied by a large oval mass called the "nucleus;" while, at its hinder end, is a "contractile vacuole," conspicuous by its regular rhythmic appearances and disappearances. Obviously, although the *Colpoda* is not a monad, it differs from one only in subordinate details. Moreover, under certain conditions, it becomes quiescent, incloses itself in a delicate case or *cyst*, and then divides into two, four, or more portions, which are eventually set free and swim about as active *Colpodæ*.

But this creature is an unmistakable animal, and full-sized *Colpodæ* may be fed as easily as one feeds chickens. It is only needful to diffuse very finely ground carmine through the water in which they live, and, in a very short time, the bodies of the *Colpodæ* are stuffed with the deeply-colored granules of the pigment.

And if this were not sufficient evidence of the animality of *Colpoda*, there comes the fact that it is even more similar to another well-known animalcule, *Paramæcium*, than it is to a monad. But *Paramæcium* is so huge a creature compared with those hitherto discussed—it reaches one-one hundred and twentieth of an inch or more in length—that there is no difficulty in making out its organization in detail; and in proving that it is not only an animal but that it is an animal which possesses a somewhat complicated organization. For example, the surface layer of its body is different in structure from the deeper parts. There are two contractile vacuoles, from each of which radiates a system of vessel-like canals; and not only is there a conical depression continuous with a tube, which serve as mouth and gullet, but the food ingested takes a definite course, and refuse is rejected from a definite region. Nothing is easier than to feed these animals, and to watch the particles of indigo or carmine accumulate at the lower end of the gullet. From this they gradually project, surrounded by a ball of water, which at length passes with a jerk, oddly simulating a gulp, into the pulpy central substance of the body, there to circulate up one side and down the other, until its contents are digested and assimilated. Nevertheless, this complex animal multiplies by division, as the monad does, and, like the monad, undergoes conjugation. It stands in the same relation to *Heteromita* on the animal side, as *Coleochæte* does on the plant side. Start from either, and such an insensible series of gradations leads to the monad that it is impossible to say at any stage of the progress—here the line between the animal and the plant must be drawn.

There is reason to think that certain organisms which pass through a monad stage of existence, such as the *Myxomycetes*, are, at one time of their lives, dependent upon external sources for their protein matter, or are animals; and, at another period, manufacture it, or are plants. And seeing that the whole progress of modern investigation is in favor of the doctrine of continuity, it is a fair and probable speculation—though only a speculation—that, as there are some plants which can manufacture protein out of such apparently intractable mineral matters as carbonic acid, water, nitrate of ammonia, metallic and earthly salts; while others need to be supplied with their carbon and nitrogen in the somewhat less raw form of tartrate of ammonia and allied compounds; so there may be yet others, as is possibly the case with the true parasitic plants, which can only manage to put together materials still better prepared—still more nearly approximated to protein—until we arrive at such organisms as the *Psorospermiæ* and the *Pan-*

* Excellently described by Stein, almost all of whose statements I have verified.

histophyton, which are as much animal as vegetable in structure, but are animal in their dependence on other organisms for their food.

The singular circumstance observed by Meyer, that the *Torula* of yeast, though an indubitable plant, still flourishes most vigorously when supplied with the complex nitrogenous substance, pepsin; the probability that the *Peronospora* is nourished directly by the protoplasm of the potato-plant; and the wonderful facts which have recently been brought to light respecting insectivorous plants, all favor this view; and tend to the conclusion that the difference between animal and plant is one of degree rather than of kind; and that the problem whether, in a given case, an organism is an animal or a plant, may be essentially insoluble.

V.

UNIVERSITIES: ACTUAL AND IDEAL.*

ELECTED by the suffrages of your four Nations, Rector of the ancient University of which you are scholars, I take the earliest opportunity which has presented itself since my restoration to health, of delivering the Address which, by long custom, is expected of the holder of my office.

My first duty in opening that Address, is to offer you my most hearty thanks for the signal honor you have conferred upon me—an honor of which, as a man unconnected with you by personal or by national ties, devoid of political distinction, and a plebeian who stands by his order, I could not have dreamed. And it was the more surprising to me, as the five-and-twenty years which have passed over my head since I reached intellectual manhood, have been largely spent in no half-hearted advocacy of doctrines which have not yet found favor in the eyes of Academic respectability; so that, when the proposal to nominate me for your Rector came, I was almost as much astonished as was Hal o' the Wynd, "who fought for his own hand," by the Black Douglas's proffer of knighthood. And I fear that my acceptance must be taken as evidence that, less wise than the Armorer of Perth, I have not yet done with soldiering.

In fact, if, for a moment, I imagined that your intention was simply, in the kindness of your hearts, to do me honor; and that the Rector of your University, like that of some other Universities, was one of those happy beings who sit in glory for three years, with nothing to do for it save the making of a speech, a conversation with my distinguished predecessor soon dispelled the dream. I found that, by the constitution of the University of Aberdeen, the incumbent of the Rectorate is, if not a power, at any rate a potential energy; and that, whatever may be his chances of success or failure, it is his duty to convert that potential energy into a living force, directed toward such ends as may seem to him conducive to the welfare of the corporation of which he is the theoretical head.

I need not tell you that your late Lord Rector took this view of his position, and acted upon it with the comprehensive, far-seeing insight into the actual condition and tendencies, not merely of his own, but of other countries, which is his honorable characteristic among statesmen. I have already done my best, and, as long as I hold my office, I shall continue my endeavors, to follow in the path which he trod; to do what in me lies, to bring this University nearer to the ideal—alas, that I should be obliged to say ideal—of all Universities; which, as I conceive, should be places in which thought is free from all fetters; and in which all sources of knowledge, and all aids to learning, should be accessible to all comers, without distinction of creed or country, riches or poverty.

Do not suppose, however, that I am sanguine enough to expect much to come of any poor efforts of mine. If your annals take any notice of my incumbency, I shall probably go down to posterity as the Rector who was always beaten. But if they add, as I think they will, that my defeats became victories in the hands of my successors, I shall be well content.

The scenes are shifting in the great theater of the world. The act which commenced with the Protestant Reformation is nearly played out, and a wider and a deeper change than that effected three centuries ago—a reformation, or rather a revolution of thought, the extremes of which are represented by the intellectual heirs of John of Leyden and of Ignatius Loyola, rather than by those of Luther and of Leo—is waiting to come on, nay, visible behind the scenes to those who have good eyes. Men are beginning, once more, to awake to the fact that matters of belief and of speculation are of absolutely infinite practical importance; and are draw-

* Address delivered by Prof. Huxley when installed as Lord Rector of Aberdeen University (1874).

ing off from that sunny country "where it is always afternoon"—the sleepy hollow of broad indifferentism—to range themselves under their natural banners. Change is in the air. It is whirling featherheads into all sorts of eccentric orbits, and filling the steadiest with a sense of insecurity. It insists on reopening all questions and asking all institutions, however venerable, by what right they exist, and whether they are, or are not, in harmony with the real or supposed wants of mankind. And it is remarkable that these searching inquiries are not so much forced on institutions from without, as developed from within. Consummate scholars question the value of learning; priests contemn dogma; and women turn their backs upon man's ideal of perfect womanhood, and seek satisfaction in apocalyptic visions of some, as yet unrealized, epicene reality.

If there be a type of stability in this world, one would be inclined to look for it in the old Universities of England. But it has been my business of late to hear a good deal about what is going on in these famous corporations; and I have been filled with astonishment by the evidences of internal fermentation which they exhibit. If Gibbon could revisit the ancient seat of learning of which he has written so cavalierly, assuredly he would no longer speak of "the monks of Oxford sunk in prejudice and port." There, as elsewhere, port has gone out of fashion, and so has prejudice—at least that particular fine, old, crusted sort of prejudice to which the great historian alludes.

Indeed, thing are moving so fast in Oxford and Cambridge, that, for my part, I rejoiced when the Royal Commission, of which I am a member, had finished and presented the Report which related to these Universities; for we should have looked like mere plagiarists, if, in consequence of a little longer delay in issuing it, all the measures of reform we proposed had been anticipated by the spontaneous action of the Universities themselves.

A month ago I should have gone on to say that one might speedily expect changes of another kind in Oxford and Cambridge. A Commission has been inquiring into the revenues of the many wealthy societies, in more or less direct connection with the Universities, resident in those towns. It is said that the Commission has reported, and that, for the first time in recorded history, the nation, and perhaps the Colleges themselves, will know what they are worth. And it was announced that a statesman, who, whatever his other merits or defects, his aims above the level of mere party fighting, and a clear vision into the most complex practical problems, meant to deal with these revenues.

But, *Bos locutus est*. That mysterious independent variable of political calculation, Public Opinion—which some whisper is, in the present case, very much the same thing as publican's opinion—has willed otherwise. The Heads may return to their wonted slumbers—at any rate for a space.

Is the spirit of change, which is working thus vigorously in the South, likely to affect the Northern Universities, and if so, to what extent? The violence of fermentation depends, not so much on the quantity of the yeast, as on the composition of the wort, and its richness in fermentable material; and, as a preliminary to the discussion of this question, I venture to call to your minds the essential and fundamental differences between the Scottish and the English type of University.

Do not charge me with anything worse than official egotism, if I say that these differences appear to be largely symbolized by my own existence. There is no Rector in an English University. Now, the organization of the members of an University into Nations, with their elective Rector, is the last relic of the primitive constitution of Universities. The Rectorate was the most important of all offices in that University of Paris, upon the model of which the University of Aberdeen was fashioned; and which was certainly a great and flourishing institution in the twelfth century.

Enthusiasts for the antiquity of one of the two acknowledged parents of all Universities, indeed, do not hesitate to trace the origin of the "Studium Parisiense" up to that wonderful king of the Franks and Lombards, Karl, surnamed the Great, whom we all called Charlemagne, and believed to be a Frenchman, until a learned historian, by beneficent iteration, taught us better. Karl is said not to have been much of a scholar himself, but he had the wisdom of which knowledge is only the servitor. And that wisdom enabled him to see that ignorance is one of the roots of all evil.

In the Capitulary which enjoins the foundation of monasterial and cathedral schools, he says: "Right action is better than knowledge; but in order to do what is right, we must know what is right." An irrefragable truth, I fancy. Acting upon it, the king took pretty full compulsory powers, and carried into effect a really considerable and effectual scheme of elementary education through the length and breadth of his dominions.

No doubt the idolaters out by the Elbe, in what is now part of Prussia, objected to the Frankish king's measures; no doubt the priests, who had never hesitated about sacrificing all unbelievers in their fantastic deities and futile conjurations, were the loudest in chanting the virtues of toleration; no doubt they denounced as a cruel persecutor the man who would not allow them, however sincere they might be, to go on spreading delusions which debased the intellect, as much as they deadened the moral sense, and undermined the bonds of civil allegiance; no doubt, if they had lived in these times, they would have been able to show, with ease, that the king's proceedings were totally contrary to the best liberal principles. But it may be said, in justification of the Teutonic ruler, first, that he was born before those principles, and did not suspect that the best way of getting disorder into order was to let it alone; and, secondly, that his rough and questionable proceedings did, more or less, bring about the end he had in view. For, in a couple of centuries, the schools he sowed broadcast produced their crop of men, thirsting for knowledge and craving for culture. Such men gravitating toward Paris, as a light amidst the darkness of evil days, from Germany, from Spain, from Britain, and from Scandinavia, came together by natural affinity. By degrees they banded themselves into a society, which, as its end was the knowledge of all things knowable, called itself a "*Studium Generale*;" and when it had grown into a recognized corporation, acquired the name of "*Universitas Studii Generalis*," which, mark you, means not a "Useful Knowledge Society," but a "Knowledge-of-things-in-general Society."

And thus the first "University," at any rate on this side of the Alps, came into being. Originally it had but one Faculty, that of Arts. Its aim was to be a center of knowledge and culture; not to be, in any sense, a technical school.

The scholars seem to have studied Grammar, Logic, and Rhetoric; Arithmetic and Geometry; Astronomy; Theology; and Music. Thus, their work, however imperfect and faulty, judged by modern lights, it may have been, brought them face to face with all the leading aspects of the many-sided mind of man. For these studies did really contain, at any rate in embryo—sometimes, it may be, in caricature—what we now call Philosophy, Mathematical and Physical Science, and Art. And I doubt if the curriculum of any modern University shows so clear and generous a comprehension of what is meant by culture, as this old Trivium and Quadrivium does.

The students who had passed through the University course, and had proved themselves competent to teach, became masters and teachers of their younger brethren. Whence the distinction of Masters and Regents on the one hand, and Scholars on the other.

Rapid growth necessitated organization. The Masters and Scholars of various tongues and countries grouped themselves into four Nations; and the Nations, by their own votes at first, and subsequently by those of their Procurators, or representatives, elected their supreme head and governor, the Rector—at that time the sole representative of the University, and a very real power, who could defy Provosts interfering from without; or could inflict even corporal punishment on disobedient members within the University.

Such was the primitive constitution of the University of Paris. It is in reference to this original state of things that I have spoken of the Rectorate, and all that appertains to it, as the sole relic of that constitution.

But this original organization did not last long. Society was not then, any more than it is now, patient of culture, as such. It says to everything, "Be useful to me, or away with you." And to the learned, the unlearned man said then, as he does now, "What is the use of all your learning, unless you can tell me what I want to know? I am here blindly groping about, and constantly damaging myself by collision with three mighty powers, the power of the invisible God, the power of my fellow Man, and the power of brute Nature. Let your learning be turned to the study of these powers, that I may know how I am to comport myself with regard to them." In answer to this demand, some of the Masters of the Faculty of Arts devoted themselves to the study of Theology, some to that of Law, and some to that of Medicine; and they became Doctors—men learned in those technical, or, as we now call them, professional, branches of knowledge. Like cleaving to like, the Doctors formed schools, or Faculties, of Theology, Law, and Medicine, which sometimes assumed airs of superiority over their parent, the Faculty of Arts, though the latter always asserted and maintained its fundamental supremacy.

The Faculties arose by process of natural differentiation out of the primitive University. Other constituents, foreign to its nature, were speedily grafted upon it. One of these extraneous elements was forced into it by the Roman Church, which in those days asserted with effect, that which it now asserts, happily without any effect in these realms, its right of censorship and control over all teaching. The local habitation of the University lay partly in the lands attached to the monastery of S. Geneviève, partly in the diocese of the Bishop of Paris; and he who would teach must have the license of the Abbot, or of the Bishop, as the nearest representative of the Pope, so to do, which license was granted by the Chancellors of these Ecclesiastics.

Thus, if I am what archæologists call a "survival" of the primitive head and ruler of the University, your Chancellor stands in the same relation to the Papacy; and, with all respect for his Grace, I think I may say that we both look terribly shrunken when compared with our great originals.

Not so is it with a second foreign element, which silently dropped into the soil of Universities, like the grain of mustard-seed in the parable; and, like that grain, grew into a tree, in whose branches a whole aviary of fowls took shelter. That element is the element of Endowment. It differed from the preceding, in its original design to serve as a prop to the young plant, not to be a parasite upon it. The charitable and the humane, blessed with wealth, were very early penetrated by the misery of the poor student. And the wise saw that intellectual ability is not so common or so unimportant a gift that it should be allowed to run to waste upon mere handicrafts and chares. The man who was a blessing to his contemporaries, but who so often has been converted into a curse, by the blind adherence of his posterity to the letter, rather than to the spirit, of his wishes—I mean the "pious founder"—gave money and lands, that the student, who was rich in brain and poor in all else, might be taken from the plough or from the stithy, and enabled to devote himself to the higher service of mankind; and built colleges and halls in which he might be not only housed and fed, but taught.

The Colleges were very generally placed in strict subordination to the University by their founders; but, in many cases, their endowment, consisting of land, has undergone an "unearned increment," which has given these societies a continually increasing weight and importance as against the unendowed, or fixedly endowed, University. In Pharaoh's dream, the seven lean kine eat up the seven fat ones. In the reality of historical fact, the fat Colleges have eaten up the lean Universities.

Even here in Aberdeen, though the causes at work may have been somewhat different, the effects have been similar; and you see how much more substantial an entity is the Very Reverend the Principal, analogue, if not homologue, of the Principals of King's College, than the Rector, lineal representative of the ancient monarchs of the University, though now, little more than a "king of shreds and patches."

Do not suppose that, in thus briefly tracing the process of University metamorphosis, I have had any intention of quarreling with its results. Practically, it seems to me that the broad changes effected in 1858 have given the Scottish Universities a very liberal constitution, with as much real approximation to the primitive state of things as is at all desirable. If your fat kine have eaten the lean, they have not lain down to chew the cud ever since. The Scottish Universities, like the English, have diverged widely enough from their primitive model; but I cannot help thinking that the northern form has remained more faithful to its original, not only in constitution, but, what is more to the purpose, in view of the cry for change, in the practical application of the endowments connected with it.

In Aberdeen, these endowments are numerous, but so small that, taken altogether, they are not equal to the revenue of a single third-rate English college. They are scholarships, not fellowships; aids to do work—not rewards for such work as it lies within the reach of an ordinary, or even an extraordinary, young man to do. You do not think that passing a respectable examination is a fair equivalent for an income, such as many a gray-headed veteran, or clergyman, would envy; and which is larger than the endowment of many Regius chairs. You do not care to make your University a school of manners for the rich; of sports for the athletic; or a hot-bed of high-fed, hypercritical refinement, more destructive to vigor and originality than are starvation and oppression. No; your little Bursaries of ten and twenty (I believe even fifty) pounds a year, enable any boy who has shown ability in the course of his education in those remarkable primary schools, which have made Scotland the power she is, to obtain the highest culture the country can give him; and when he is armed and equipped, his Spartan Alma Mater tells him that, so far, he has had his wages for his work, and that he may go and earn the rest.

When I think of the host of pleasant, monied, well-bred young gentlemen, who do a little learning and much boating by Cam and Isis, the vision is a pleasant one; and, as a patriot, I rejoice that the youth of the upper and richer classes of the nation receive a wholesome and a manly training, however small may be the modicum of knowledge they gather, in the intervals of this, their serious business. I admit, to the full, the social and political value of that training. But, when I proceed to consider that these young men may be said to represent the great bulk of what the Colleges have to show for their enormous wealth, plus, at least, a hundred and fifty pounds a year apiece which each undergraduate costs his parents or guardians, I feel inclined to ask, whether the rate-in-aid of the education of the wealthy and professional classes, thus levied on the resources of the community, is not, after all, a little heavy? And, still further, I am tempted to inquire what has become of the indigent scholars, the sons of the masses of the people whose daily labor just suffices to meet their daily wants, for whose benefit these rich foundations were largely, if not mainly, instituted? It seems as if Pharaoh's dream had been rigorously carried out, and that even the fat scholar has eaten the lean one. And when I turn from this picture to the no less real vision of many a brave and frugal Scotch boy, spending his summer in hard manual labor, that he may have the privilege of wending his way in autumn to this University, with a bag of oatmeal, ten pounds in his pocket, and his own stout heart to depend upon through the northern winter; not bent on seeking

"The bubble reputation at the cannon's mouth,"

but determined to wring knowledge from the hard hands of penury; when I see him win through all such outward obstacles to positions of wide usefulness and well-earned fame; I cannot but think that, in essence, Aberdeen has departed but little from the primitive intention of the founders of Universities, and that the spirit of reform has so much to do on the other side of the Border, that it may be long before he has leisure to look this way.

As compared with other actual Universities, then, Aberdeen, may, perhaps, be well satisfied with itself. But do not think me an impracticable dreamer, if I ask you not to rest and be thankful in this state of satisfaction; if I ask you to consider awhile, how this actual good stands related to that ideal better, towards which both men and institutions must progress, if they would not retrograde.

In an ideal University, as I conceive it, a man should be able to obtain instruction in all forms of knowledge, and discipline in the use of all the methods by which knowledge is obtained. In such an University, the force of living example should fire the student with a noble ambition to emulate the learning of learned men, and to follow in the footsteps of the explorers of new fields of knowledge. And the very air he breathes should be charged with that enthusiasm for truth, that fanaticism of veracity, which is a greater possession than much learning; a nobler gift than the power of increasing knowledge; by so much greater and nobler than these, as the moral nature of man is greater than the intellectual; for veracity is the heart of morality.

But the man who is all morality and intellect, although he may be good and even great, is, after all, only half a man. There is beauty in the moral world and in the intellectual world; but there is also a beauty which is neither moral nor intellectual—the beauty of the world of Art. There are men who are devoid of the power of seeing it, as there are men who are born deaf and blind, and the loss of those, as of these, is simply infinite. There are others in whom it is an overpowering passion; happy men, born with the productive, or at lowest, the appreciative, genius of the Artist. But, in the mass of mankind, the Æsthetic faculty, like the reasoning power and the moral sense, needs to be roused, directed, and cultivated; and I know not why the development of that side of his nature, through which man has access to a perennial spring of ennobling pleasure, should be omitted from any comprehensive scheme of University education.

All Universities recognize Literature in the sense of the old Rhetoric, which is art incarnate in words. Some, to their credit, recognize Art in its narrower sense, to a certain extent, and confer degrees for proficiency in some of its branches. If there are Doctors of Music, why should there be no Masters of Painting, of Sculpture, of Architecture? I should like to see Professors of the Fine Arts in every University; and instruction in some branch of their work made a part of the Arts curriculum.

I just now expressed the opinion that, in our ideal University, a man should be able to obtain instruction in all forms of knowledge. Now, by "forms of knowledge" I mean the great classes of things knowable; of which the first, in logical, though not in natural, order is knowledge relating to the scope and limits of the mental faculties of man; a form of knowledge which, in its positive aspect, answers pretty much to Logic and part of Psychology, while, on its negative and critical side, it corresponds with Metaphysics.

A second class comprehends all that knowledge which relates to man's welfare, so far as it is determined by his own acts, or what we call his conduct. It answers to Moral and Religious philosophy. Practically, it is the most directly valuable of all forms of knowledge, but speculatively, it is limited and criticised by that which precedes and by that which follows it in my order of enumeration.

A third class embraces knowledge of the phenomena of the Universe, as that which lies about the individual man: and of the rules which those phenomena are observed to follow in the order of their occurrence, which we term the laws of Nature.

This is what ought to be called Natural Science, or Physiology, though those terms are hopelessly diverted from such a meaning; and it includes all exact knowledge of natural fact, whether Mathematical, Physical, Biological, or Social.

Kant has said that the ultimate object of all knowledge is to give replies to these three questions: What can I do? What ought I to do? What may I hope for? The forms of knowledge which I have enumerated, should furnish such replies as are within human reach, to the first and second of these questions. While to the third, perhaps the wisest answer is, "Do what you can to do what you ought, and leave hoping and fearing alone."

If this be a just and an exhaustive classification of the forms of knowledge, no question as to their relative importance, or as to the superiority of one to the other, can be seriously raised.

On the face of the matter, it is absurd to ask whether it is more important to know the limits of one's powers; or the ends for which they ought to be exerted; or the conditions under which they must be exerted. One may as well inquire which of the terms of a Rule of Three sum one ought to know, in order to get a trustworthy result. Practical life is such a sum, in which your duty multiplied into your capacity, and divided by your circumstances, gives you the fourth term in the proportion, which is your deserts, with great accuracy. All agree, I take it, that men ought to have these three kinds of knowledge. The so-called "conflict of studies" turns upon the question of how they may best be obtained.

The founders of Universities held the theory that the Scriptures and Aristotle taken together, the latter being limited by the former, contained all knowledge worth having; and that the business of philosophy was to interpret and co-ordinate these two. I imagine that in the twelfth century this was a very fair conclusion from known facts. Nowhere in the world, in those days, was there such an encyclopedia of knowledge of all three classes, as is to be found in those writings. The scholastic philosophy is a wonderful monument of the patience and ingenuity with which the human mind toiled to build up a logically consistent theory of the Universe, out of such materials. And that philosophy is by no means dead and buried, as many vainly suppose. On the contrary, numbers of men of no mean learning and accomplishment, and sometimes of rare power and subtlety of thought, hold by it as the best theory of things which has yet been stated. And, what is still more remarkable, men who speak the language of modern philosophy, nevertheless think the thoughts of the schoolmen. "The voice is the voice of Jacob, but the hands are the hands of Esau." Every day I hear "Cause," "Law," "Force," "Vitality," spoken of as entities, by people who can enjoy Swift's joke about the meat-roasting quality of the smoke-jack, and comfort themselves with the reflection that they are not even as those benighted schoolmen.

Well, this great system had its day, and then it was sapped and mined by two influences. The first was the study of classical literature, which familiarized men with methods of philosophizing; with conceptions of the highest Good; with ideas of the order of Nature; with notions of Literary and Historical Criticism; and above all, with visions of Art, of a kind which not only would not fit into the scholastic scheme, but showed them a pre-Christian, and indeed altogether un-Christian world, of such grandeur and beauty that they ceased to think of any other. They were as men who had kissed the Fairy Queen, and wandering with her in the dim loveliness of the under-world, cared not to return to the familiar ways of home and fatherland, though they lay, at arm's length, overhead. Cardinals were more familiar with Virgil than with Isaiah; and Popes labored, with great success, to re-paganize Rome.

The second influence was the slow, but sure, growth of the physical sciences. It was discovered that some results of speculative thought, of immense practical and theoretical importance, can be verified by observation; and are always true, however severely they may be tested. Here, at any rate, was knowledge, to the certainty of which no authority could add, or take away, one jot or tittle, and to which the tradition of a thousand years was as insignificant as the hearsay of yesterday. To the scholastic system, the study of classical literature might be inconvenient and distracting, but it was possible to hope that it could be kept within bounds. Physical science, on the other hand, was an irreconcilable enemy, to be excluded at all hazards. The College of Cardinals has not distinguished itself in Physics or Physiology; and no Pope has, as yet, set up public laboratories in the Vatican.

People do not always formulate the beliefs on which they act. The instinct of fear and dislike is quicker than the reasoning process; and I suspect that, taken in conjunction with some other causes, such instinctive aversion is at the bottom of the long exclusion of any serious discipline in the physical sciences from the general curriculum of Universities; while, on the other hand, classical literature has been gradually made the backbone of the Arts course.

I am ashamed to repeat here what I have said elsewhere, in season and out of season, respecting the value of Science as knowledge and discipline. But the other day I met with some passages in the Address to another Scottish University, of a great thinker, recently lost to us, which express so fully, and yet so tersely, the truth in this matter, that I am fain to quote them :—

"To question all things;—never to turn away from any difficulty; to accept no doctrine either from ourselves or from other people without a rigid scrutiny by negative criticism; letting no fallacy, or incoherence, or confusion of thought step by unperceived; above all, to insist upon having the meaning of a word clearly understood before using it, and the meaning of a proposition before assenting to it;—these are the lessons we learn" from workers in Science. "With all this vigorous management of the negative element, they inspire no scepticism about the reality of truth or indifference to its pursuit. The noblest enthusiasm, both for the search after truth and for applying it to its highest uses, pervades those writers." "In cultivating, therefore," science as an essential ingredient in education, "we are all the while laying an admirable foundation for ethical and philosophical culture." *

The passages I have quoted were uttered by John Stuart Mill; but you cannot hear inverted commas, and it is therefore right that I should add, without delay, that I have taken the liberty of substituting "workers in science" for "ancient dialecticians," and "Science as an essential ingredient in education" for "the ancient languages as our best literary education." Mill did, in fact, deliver a noble panegyric upon classical studies. I do not doubt its justice, nor presume to question its wisdom. But I venture to maintain that no wise or just judge, who has a knowledge of the facts, will hesitate to say that it applies with equal force to scientific training.

But it is only fair to the Scottish Universities to point out that they have long understood the value of Science as a branch of general education. I observe, with the greatest satisfaction, that candidates for the degree of Master of Arts in this University are required to have a knowledge, not only of Mental and Moral Philosophy, and of Mathematics and Natural Philosophy, but of Natural History, in addition to the ordinary Latin and Greek course; and that a candidate may take honors in these subjects and in Chemistry.

I do not know what the requirements of your examiners may be, but I sincerely trust they are not satisfied with a mere book knowledge of these matters. For my own part, I would not raise a finger, if I could thereby introduce mere book work in science into every Arts curriculum in the country. Let those who want to study books devote themselves to Literature, in which we have the perfection of books, both as to substance and as to form.

*** Inaugural Address delivered to the University of St. Andrews, February 1, 1867, by J. S. Mill, Rector of the University (pp. 32, 33).**

If I may paraphrase Hobbes's well-known aphorism, I would say that "books are the money of Literature, but only the counters of Science," Science (in the sense in which I now use the term) being the knowledge of fact, of which every verbal description is but an incomplete and symbolic expression. And be assured that no teaching of science is worth anything, as a mental discipline, which is not based upon direct perception of the facts, and practical exercise of the observing and logical faculties upon them. Even in such a simple matter as the mere comprehension of form, ask the most practiced and widely informed anatomist what is the difference between his knowledge of a structure which he has read about, and his knowledge of the same structure when he has seen it for himself; and he will tell you that the two things are not comparable—the difference is infinite. Thus I am very strongly inclined to agree with some learned schoolmasters who say that, in their experience, the teaching of science is all waste time. As they teach it, I have no doubt it is. But to teach it otherwise, requires an amount of personal labor and a development of means and appliances, which must strike horror and dismay into a man accustomed to mere book work; and who has been in the habit of teaching a class of fifty without much strain upon his energies. And this is one of the real difficulties in the way of the introduction of physical science into the ordinary University course, to which I have alluded. It is a difficulty which will not be overcome, until years of patient study have organized scientific teaching as well as, or I hope better than, classical teaching has been organized hitherto.

A little while ago, I ventured to hint a doubt as to the perfection of some of the arrangements in the ancient Universities of England; but, in their provision for giving instruction in Science as such, and without direct reference to any of its practical applications, they have set a brilliant example. Within the last twenty years, Oxford alone has sunk more than a hundred and twenty thousand pounds in building and furnishing Physical, Chemical, and Physiological Laboratories, and a magnificent Museum, arranged with an almost luxurious regard for the needs of the student. Cambridge, less rich, but aided by the munificence of her Chancellor, is taking the same course; and, in a few years, it will be for no lack of the means and appliances of sound teaching, if the mass of English University men remain in their present state of barbarous ignorance of even the rudiments of scientific culture.

Yet another step needs to be made before Science can be said to have taken its proper place in the Universities. That is its recognition as a Faculty, or branch of study demanding recognition and special organization, on account of its bearing on the wants of mankind. The Faculties of Theology, Law, and Medicine, are technical schools, intended to equip men who have received general culture, with the special knowledge which is needed for the proper performance of the duties of clergymen, lawyers, and medical practitioners.

When the material well-being of the country depended upon rude pasture and agriculture, and still ruder mining; in the days when all the innumerable applications of the principles of physical science to practical purposes were non-existent even as dreams; days which men living may have heard their fathers speak of; what little physical science could be seen to bear directly upon human life, lay within the province of Medicine. Medicine was the foster-mother of Chemistry, because it has to do with the preparation of drugs and the detection of poisons; of Botany, because it enabled the physician to recognize medicinal herbs; of Comparative Anatomy and Physiology, because the man who studied Human Anatomy and Physiology for purely medical purposes was led to extend his studies to the rest of the animal world.

Within my recollection, the only way in which a student could obtain anything like a training in Physical Science, was by attending the lectures of the Professors of Physical and Natural science attached to the Medical Schools. But, in the course of the last thirty years, both foster-mother and child have grown so big, that they threaten not only to crush one another, but to press the very life out of the unhappy student who enters the nursery; to the great detriment of all three.

I speak in the presence of those who know practically what medical education is; for I may assume that a large proportion of my hearers are more or less advanced students of medicine. I appeal to the most industrious and conscientious among you, to those who are most deeply penetrated with a sense of the extremely serious responsibilities which attach to the calling of a medical practitioner, when I ask whether, out of the four years which you devote to your studies, you ought to spare even so much as an hour for any work which does not tend directly to fit you for your duties?

Consider what that work is. Its foundation is a sound and practical acquaintance with the structure of the human organism, and with the modes and conditions of its action in health. I say a sound and practical acquaintance, to guard against the supposition that my intention is to suggest that you ought all to be minute anatomists and accomplished physiologists. The devotion of your whole four years to Anatomy and Physiology alone, would be totally insufficient to attain that end. What I mean is, the sort of practical, familiar, finger-end knowledge which a watchmaker has of a watch, and which you expect that craftsman, as an honest man, to have, when you entrust a watch that goes badly, to him. It is a kind of knowledge which is to be acquired, not in the lecture-room, nor in the library, but in the dissecting-room and the laboratory. It is to be had, not by sharing your attention between these and sundry other subjects, but by concentrating your minds, week after week, and month after month, six or seven hours a day, upon all the complexities of organ and function, until each of the greater truths of anatomy and physiology has become an organic part of your minds—until you would know them if you were roused and questioned in the middle of the night, as a man knows the geography of his native place and the daily life of his home. That is the sort of knowledge which, once obtained, is a life-long possession. Other occupations may fill your minds—it may grow dim, and seem to be forgotten—but there it is, like the inscription on a battered and defaced coin, which comes out when you warm it.

If I had the power to remodel Medical Education, the first two years of the medical curriculum should be devoted to nothing but such thorough study of Anatomy and Physiology, with Physiological Chemistry and Physics; the student should then pass a real, practical examination in these subjects; and, having gone through that ordeal satisfactorily, he should be troubled no more with them. His whole mind should then be given with equal intentness, to Therapeutics, in its broadest sense, to Practical Medicine and to Surgery, with instruction in Hygiene and in Medical Jurisprudence; and of these subjects only—surely there are enough of them—should he be required to show a knowledge in his final examination.

I cannot claim any special property in this theory of what the medical curriculum should be, for I find that views, more or less closely approximating these, are held by all who have seriously considered the very grave and pressing question of Medical Reform; and have, indeed, been carried into practice, to some extent, by the most enlightened Examining Boards. I have heard but two kinds of objections to them. There is, first, the objection of vested interests, which I will not deal with here, because I want to make myself as pleasant as I can, and no discussions are so unpleasant as those which turn on such points. And there is, secondly, the much more respectable objection, which takes the general form of the reproach that, in thus limiting the curriculum, we are seeking to narrow it. We are told that the medical man ought to be a person of good education and general information, if his profession is to hold its own among other professions; that he ought to know Botany, or else, if he goes abroad, he will not be able to tell poisonous fruits from edible ones; that he ought to know drugs, as a druggist knows them, or he will not be able to tell sham bark and senna from the real articles; that he ought to know Zoology, because—well, I really have never been able to learn exactly why he is to be expected to know zoology. There is, indeed, a popular superstition, that doctors know all about things that are queer or nasty to the general mind, and may, therefore, be reasonably expected to know the "barbarous binomials" applicable to snakes, snails, and slugs; an amount of information with which the general mind is usually completely satisfied. And there is a scientific superstition that Physiology is largely aided by Comparative Anatomy—a superstition which, like most superstitions, once had a grain of truth at bottom; but the grain has become homœpathic, since Physiology took its modern experimental development, and became what it is now, the application of the principles of Physics and Chemistry to the elucidation of the phenomena of life.

I hold as strongly as any one can do, that the medical practitioner ought to be a person of education and good general culture; but I also hold by the old theory of a Faculty, that a man should have his general culture before he devotes himself to the special studies of that Faculty; and I venture to maintain, that, if the general culture obtained in the Faculty of Arts were what it ought to be, the student would have quite as much knowledge of the fundamental principles of Physics, of Chemistry, and of Biology, as he needs, before he commenced his special medical studies.

Moreover, I would urge, that a thorough study of Human Physiology is, in itself, an education broader and more comprehensive than much that passes under that name. There is no side of the intellect which it does not call into play, no region of human knowledge into which either its roots, or its branches, do not extend; like the Atlantic between the Old and the New Worlds, its waves wash the shores of the two worlds of matter and of mind; its tributary streams flow from both; through its waters, as yet unfurrowed by the keel of any Columbus, lies the road, if such there be, from the one to the other; far away from that North-west Passage of mere speculation in which so many brave souls have been hopelessly frozen up.

But whether I am right or wrong about all this, the patent fact of the limitation of time remains. As the song runs:—

> "If a man could be sure
> That his life would endure
> For the space of a thousand long years——"

he might do a number of things not practicable under present conditions. Methuselah might, with much propriety, have taken half a century to get his doctor's degree; and might, very fairly, have been required to pass a practical examination upon the contents of the British Museum, before commencing practice as a promising young fellow of two hundred, or thereabouts. But you have four years to do your work in, and are turned loose, to save or slay, at two or three and twenty.

Now, I put it to you, whether you think that, when you come down to the realities of life—when you stand by the sick-bed, racking your brains for the principles which shall furnish you with the means of interpreting symptoms, and forming a rational theory of the condition of your patient, it will be satisfactory for you to find that those principles are not there—although, to use the examination slang which is unfortunately too familiar to me, you can quite easily "give an account of the leading peculiarities of the *Marsupialia*," or "enumerate the chief characters of the *Compositæ*," or "state the class and order of the animal from which Castoreum is obtained."

I really do not think that state of things will be satisfactory to you; I am very sure it will not be so to your patient. Indeed, I am so narrow-minded myself, that if I had to choose between two physicians—one who did not know whether a whale is a fish or not, and could not tell gentian from ginger, but did understand the applications of the institutes of medicine to his art; while the other, like Talleyrand's doctor, "knew everything, even a little physic"—with all my love for breadth of culture, I should assuredly consult the former.

It is not pleasant to incur the suspicion of an inclination to injure or depreciate particular branches of knowledge. But the fact that one of those which I should have no hesitation in excluding from the medical curriculum, is that to which my own life has been specially devoted, should, at any rate, defend me from the suspicion of being urged to this course by any but the very gravest considerations of the public welfare.

And I should like, further, to call your attention to the important circumstance that, in thus proposing the exclusion of the study of such branches of knowledge as Zoology and Botany, from those compulsory upon the medical student, I am not, for a moment, suggesting their exclusion from the University. I think that sound and practical instruction in the elementary facts and broad principles of Biology should form part of the Arts Curriculum: and here, happily, my theory is in entire accordance with your practice. Moreover, as I have already said, I have no sort of doubt that, in view of the relation of Physical Science to the practical life of the present day, it has the same right as Theology, Law, and Medicine, to a Faculty of its own in which men shall be trained to be professional men of science. It may be doubted whether Universities are the places for technical schools of Engineering, or Applied Chemistry, or Agriculture. But there can surely be little question, that instruction in the branches of Science which lie at the foundation of these Arts, of a far more advanced and special character than could, with any propriety, be included in the ordinary Arts Curriculum, ought to be obtainable by means of a duly organized Faculty of Science in every University.

The establishment of such a Faculty would have the additional advantage of providing, in some measure, for one of the greatest wants of our time and country. I mean the proper support and encouragement of original research.

The other day, an emphatic friend of

mine committed himself to the opinion that, in England, it is better for a man's worldly prospects to be a drunkard, than to be smitten with the divine dipsomania of the original investigator. I am inclined to think he was not far wrong. And, be it observed, that the question is not, whether such a man shall be able to make as much out of his abilities as his brother, of like ability, who goes into Law, or Engineering, or Commerce; it is not a question of "maintaining a due number of saddle horses," as George Eliot somewhere puts it—it is a question of living or starving.

If a student of my own subject shows power and originality, I dare not advise him to adopt a scientific career; for, supposing he is able to maintain himself until he has attained distinction, I cannot give him the assurance that any amout of proficiency in the Biological Sciences will be convertible into, even the most modest, bread and cheese. And I believe that the case is as bad, or perhaps worse, with other branches of Science. In this respect Britain, whose immense wealth and prosperity hang upon the thread of Applied Science, is far behind France, and infinitely behind Germany.

And the worst of it is, that it is very difficult to see one's way to any immediate remedy for this state of affairs which shall be free from a tendency to become worse than the disease.

Great schemes for the Endowment of Research have been proposed. It has been suggested, that Laboratories for all branches of Physical Science, provided with every apparatus needed by the investigator, shall be established by the State: and shall be accessible, under due conditions and regulations, to all properly qualified persons. I see no objection to the principle of such a proposal. If it be legitimate to spend great sums of money on public Libraries and public collections of Painting and Sculpture, in aid of the men of letters, or the Artist, or for the mere sake of affording pleasure to the general public, I apprehend that it cannot be illegitimate to do as much for the promotion of scientific investigation. To take the lowest ground as a mere investment of money, the latter is likely to be much more immediately profitable. To my mind, the difficulty in the way of such schemes is not theoretical, but practical. Given the laboratories, how are the investigators to be maintained? What career is open to those who have been thus encouraged to leave bread-winning pursuits? If they are to be provided for by endowment, we come back to the College Fellowship system, the results of which, for Literature, have not been so brilliant that one would wish to see it extended to Science; unless some much better securities, than at present exist, can be taken that it will foster real work. You know that among the Bees, it depends on the kind of cell in which the egg is deposited, and the quantity and quality of food which is supplied to the grub, whether it shall turn out a busy little worker or a big idle queen. And, in the human hive, the cells of the endowed larvæ are always tending to enlarge, and their food to improve, until we get queens, beautiful to behold, but which gather no honey and build no comb.

I do not say that these difficulties may not be overcome, but their gravity is not to be lightly estimated.

In the mean while, there is one step in the direction of the endowment of research which is free from such objections. It is possible to place the scientific inquirer in a position in which he shall have ample leisure and opportunity for original work, and yet shall give a fair and tangible equivalent for those privileges. The establishment of a Faculty of Science in every University, implies that of a corresponding number of Professorial chairs, the incumbents of which need not be so burdened with teaching as to deprive them of ample leisure for original work. I do not think that it is any impediment to an original investigator to have to devote a moderate portion of his time to lecturing, or superintending practical instruction. On the contrary, I think it may be, and often is, a benefit to be obliged to take a comprehensive survey of your subject; or to bring your results to a point, and give them, as it were, a tangible objective existence. The besetting sins of the investigator are two: the one is the desire to put aside a subject, the general bearings of which he has mastered himself, and pass on to something which has the attraction of novelty, and the other, the desire for too much perfection, which leads him to

> "Add and alter many times,
> Till all be ripe and rotten;"

to spend the energies which should be reserved for action, in whitening the decks and polishing the guns.

But supposing the Professorial forces of our University to be duly organized, there remains an important question, relating to the teaching power, to be considered. Is the Professorial system—the system, I mean, of teaching in the lecture-room alone, and leaving the student to find his own way when he is outside the lecture-room—adequate to the wants of learners? In answering this question, I confine myself to my own province, and I venture to reply for Physical Science, assuredly and undoubtedly, No. As I have already intimated. practical work in the Laboratory is absolutely indispensable, and that practical work must be guided and superintended by a sufficient staff of Demonstrators, who are for Science what Tutors are for other branches of study. And there must be a good supply of such Demonstrators. I doubt if the practical work of more than twenty students can be properly superintended by one Demonstrator. If we take the working day at six hours, that is less than twenty minutes apiece—not a very large allowance of time for helping a dull man, for correcting an inaccurate one, or even for making an intelligent student clearly apprehend what he is about. And, no doubt, the supplying of a proper amount of this tutorial, practical teaching, is a difficulty in the way of giving proper instruction in Physical Science in such Universities as that of Aberdeen, which are devoid of endowments; and, unlike the English Universities, have no claim on the funds of richly endowed bodies to supply their wants.

Examination—thorough, searching examination—is an indispensable accompaniment of teaching; but I am almost inclined to commit myself to the very heterodox proposition that it is a necessary evil. I am a very old Examiner, having, for some twenty years past, been occupied with examinations on a considerable scale, of all sorts and conditions of men, and women too,—from the boys and girls of elementary schools to the candidates for Honors and Fellowships in the Universities. I will not say that, in this case as in so many others, the adage, that familiarity breeds contempt, holds good; but my admiration for the existing system of examination and its products, does not wax warmer as I see more of it. Examination, like fire, is a good servant, but a bad master; and there seems to be some danger of its becoming our master. I by no means stand alone in this opinion. Experienced friends of mine do not hesitate to say that students whose career they watch, appear to them to become deteriorated by the constant effort to pass this or that examination, just as we hear of men's brains becoming affected by the daily necessity of catching a train. They work to pass, not to know; and outraged Science takes her revenge. They do pass, and they don't know. I have passed sundry examinations in my time, not without credit, and I confess I am ashamed to think how very little real knowledge underlay the torrent of stuff which I was able to pour out on paper. In fact, that which examination, as ordinarily conducted, tests, is simply a man's power of work under stimulus, and his capacity for rapidly and clearly producing that which, for the time, he has got into his mind. Now, these faculties are by no means to be despised. They are of great value in practical life, and are the making of many an advocate, and of many a so-called statesman. But in the pursuit of truth, scientific or other, they count for very little, unless they are supplemented by that long-continued, patient "intending of the mind," as Newton phrased it, which makes very little show in Examinations. I imagine that an Examiner who knows his students personally, must not unfrequently have found himself in the position of finding A's paper better than B's, though his own judgment tells him, quite clearly, that B is the man who has the larger share of genuine capacity.

Again, there is a fallacy about Examiners. It is commonly supposed that any one who knows a subject is competent to teach it; and no-one seems to doubt that any one who knows a subject is competent to examine in it. I believe both these opinions to be serious mistakes: the latter, perhaps, the more serious of the two. In the first place, I do not believe that any one who is not, or has not been, a teacher is really qualified to examine advanced students. In the second place, Examination is an Art, and a difficult one, which has to be learned like all other arts.

Beginners always set too difficult questions—partly because they are afraid of being suspected of ignorance if they set easy ones, and partly from not understanding their business. Suppose that you want to test the relative physical strength of a score of young men. You do not put a hundredweight down before them, and tell each to swing it round. If you do, half of them won't be able to lift it at all, and only one or two will be able to perform the task. You must give them half a hundredweight, and see how they maneuver that, if you want to form any estimate of the muscular strength of each. So, a practiced Examiner will seek for information respecting the mental vigor and training of candidates from the way in which they deal with questions easy enough to let reason, memory, and method have free play.

No doubt, a great deal is to be done by the careful selection of Examiners, and by the copious introduction of practical work, to remove the evils inseparable from examination; but, under the best of circumstances, I believe that examination will remain but an imperfect test of knowledge, and a still more imperfect test of capacity, while it tells next to nothing about a man's power as an investigator.

There is much to be said in favor of restricting the highest degress in each Faculty, to those who have shown evidence of such original power, by prosecuting a research under the eye of the Professor in whose province it lies; or, at any rate, under conditions which shall afford satisfactory proof that the work is theirs. The notion may sound revolutionary, but it is really very old; for, I take it, that it lies at the bottom of that presentation of a thesis by the candidate for a doctorate, which has now, too often, become little better than a matter of form.

Thus far, I have endeavored to lay before you, in a too brief and imperfect manner, my views respecting the teaching half—the Magistri and Regentes—of the University of the Future. Now let me turn to the learning half—the Scholares.

If the Universities are to be the sanctuaries of the highest culture of the country, those who would enter that sanctuary, must not come with unwashed hands. If the good seed is to yield its hundredfold harvest, it must not be scattered amidst the stones of ignorance, or the tares of undisciplined indolence and wantonness. On the contrary, the soil must have been carefully prepared, and the Professor should find that the operations of clod-crushing, draining, and weeding, and even a good deal of planting, have been done by the Schoolmaster.

That is exactly what the Professor does not find in any University in the three Kingdoms that I can hear of—the reason of which state of things lies in the extremely faulty organization of the majority of secondary Schools. Students come to the Universities ill-prepared in classics and mathematics, not at all prepared in anything else; and half their time is spent in learning that which they ought to have known when they came.

I sometimes hear it said that the Scottish Universities differ from the English, in being to a much greater extent places of comparatively elementary education for a younger class of students. But it would seem doubtful if any great difference of this kind really exists; for a high authority, himself Head of an English College, has solemnly affirmed that: "Elementary teaching of youths under twenty is now the only function performed by the University;" and that Colleges are "boarding schools in which the elements of the learned languages are taught to youth." *

This is not the first time that I have quoted those remarkable assertions. I should like to engrave them in public view, for they have not been refuted; and I am convinced that if their import is once clearly apprehended, they will play no mean part when the question of University reorganization, with a view to practical measures, comes on for discussion. You are not responsible for this anomalous state of affairs now; but, as you pass into active life and acquire the political influence to which your education and your position should entitle you, you will become responsible for it, unless each in his sphere does his best to alter it, by insisting on the improvement of secondary Schools.

Your present responsibility is of another, though not less serious, kind. Institutions do not make men, any more than organization makes life; and even the ideal University we have been dreaming about will be but a superior piece of mechanism, unless each student strive after the ideal of the Scholar. And that ideal, it seems to me, has never been better embodied than by the great Poet, who, though lapped in luxury, the favorite of a Court, and the idol of his countrymen, remained through all the length of his honored years a Scholar in Art, in Science, and in Life.

Would'st shape a noble life? Then cast
No backward glances toward the past:
And though somewhat be lost and gone,
Yet do thou act as one new-born.
What each day needs, that shalt thou ask;
Each day will set its proper task.
Give other's work just share of praise;
Not of thine own the merits raise.
Beware no fellow man thou hate:
And so in God's hands leave thy fate.†

* "Suggestions for Academical Organization, with Especial Reference to Oxford." By the Rector of Lincoln.

† Goethe, *Zahme Xenien*, *Vierte Abtheilung* I should be glad to take credit for the close and vigorous English version; but it is my wife's, and not mine.

CONTENTS.

TEN BOOKS FOR THE PRICE OF ONE.

The Humboldt Library of Science

Is the only publication of its kind, the only one containing *popular scientific works at low prices*. For the most part it contains only *works of acknowledged excellence*, by authors of the first rank in the world of science.
In this series are well represented the writings of

DARWIN, HUXLEY, SPENCER, TYNDALL, PROCTOR,
CLIFFORD, CLODD, BAGEHOT, BAIN, BATES,
WALLACE, TRENCH, ROMANES, GRANT ALLEN, GEIKIE,
HINTON, SULLY, FLAMMARION, PICTON, WILLIAMS,
BALFOUR STEWART, WILSON,

And other leaders of thought in our time. The books are Complete and Unabridged Editions, in Neat Paper Covers.

Price, FIFTEEN Cents a Number. Double Numbers, THIRTY Cents.

No. 1. **Light Science for Leisure Hours.** A series of familiar essays on astronomical and other natural phenomena. By Richard A. Proctor, F.R.A.S.

No. 2. **Forms of Water** in Clouds and Rivers, Ice and Glaciers. (*19 illustrations*). By John Tyndall, F.R.S.

No. 3. **Physics and Politics.** An application of the principles of Natural Science to Political Society. By Walter Bagehot, author of "The English Constitution."

No. 4. **Man's Place in Nature,** (*with numerous illustrations*). By Thomas H. Huxley, F.R.S.

No. 5. **Education,** Intellectual, Moral, and Physical. By Herbert Spencer.

No. 6. **Town Geology.** With Appendix on Coral and Coral Reefs. By Rev. Chas. Kingsley.

No. 7. **The Conservation of Energy,** (*with numerous illustrations*). By Balfour Stewart, LL.D.

No. 8. **The Study of Languages,** brought back to its true principles. By C. Marcel.

No. 9. **The Data of Ethics.** By Herbert Spencer.

No. 10. **The Theory of Sound in its Relation to Music,** (*numerous illustrations*). By Prof. Pietro Blaserna.

No. 11. / No. 12. **The Naturalist on the River Amazon.** A record of 11 years of travel. By Henry Walton Bates, F.L.S. (Double number. *Not sold separately*).

No. 13. **Mind and Body.** The theories of their relation. By Alex. Bain, LL.D.

No. 14. **The Wonders of the Heavens,** (*thirty-two illustrations*). By Camille Flammarion.

No. 15. **Longevity.** The means of prolonging life after middle age. By John Gardner, M.D.

No. 16. **On the Origin of Species.** By Thomas H. Huxley, F.R.S.

No. 17. **Progress: Its Law and Cause.** With other disquisitions. By Herbert Spencer.

No. 18. **Lessons in Electricity,** (*sixty illustrations*). By John Tyndall, F.R.S.

No. 19. **Familiar Essays on Scientific Subjects.** By Richard A. Proctor.

No. 20. **The Romance of Astronomy.** By R. Kalley Miller, M.A.

No. 21. **The Physical Basis of Life,** with other essays. By Thomas H. Huxley, F.R.S.

No. 22. **Seeing and Thinking.** By William Kingdon Clifford, F.R.S.

No. 23. **Scientific Sophisms.** A review of current theories concerning Atoms, Apes and Men. By Samuel Wainwright, D.D.

No. 24. **Popular Scientific Lectures,** (*illustrated*). By Prof. H. Helmholtz.

No. 25. **The Origin of Nations.** By Prof. Geo. Rawlinson, Oxford University.

No. 26. **The Evolutionist at Large.** By Grant Allen.

No. 27. **The History of Landholding in England.** By Joseph Fisher, F.R.H.S.

No. 28. **Fashion in Deformity,** as illustrated in the customs of Barbarous and Civilized Races, (*numerou illustrations*). By William Henry Flower, F.R.S.

No. 29. **Facts and Fictions of Zoology,** (*numerous illustrations*). By Andrew Wilson, Ph. D.

No. 30. **The Study of Words.** Part I. By Richard Chenevix Trench.

No. 31. **The Study of Words.** Part II.

No. 32. **Hereditary Traits and Other Essays.** By Richard A. Proctor.

No. 33. **Vignettes from Nature.** By Grant Allen.

No. 34. **The Philosophy of Style.** By Herbert Spencer.

No. 35. **Oriental Religions.** By John Caird, Pres. Univ. Glasgow, and Others.

No. 36. **Lectures on Evolution.** (*Illustrated*). By Prof. T. H. Huxley.

No. 37. **Six Lectures on Light.** (*Illustrated*). By Prof. Tyndall.

No. 38. **Geological Sketches.** Part I. By Archibald Geikie, F.R.S.

No. 39. **Geological Sketches.** Part II.

No. 40. **The Evidence of Organic Evolution.** By George J. Romanes, F.R.S.

No. 41. **Current Discussion in Science.** By W. M. Williams, F.C.S.

No. 42. **History of the Science of Politics.** By Frederick Pollock.

No. 43. **Darwin and Humboldt.** By Prof. Huxley, Prof. Agassiz, and others.

No. 44. **The Dawn of History.** Part I. By G. F. Keary, of the British Museum.

No. 45. **The Dawn of History.** Part II.

No. 46. **The Diseases of Memory.** By Th. Ribot. Translated from the French by J. Fitzgerald, M.A.

No. 47. **The Childhood of Religion.** By Edward Clodd, F.R.A.S.

No. 48. **Life in Nature.** (*Illustrated*). By James Hinton.

No. 49. **The Sun:** its Constitution, its Phenomena, its Condition. By Judge Nathan T. Carr.

No. 50. **Money and the Mechanism of Exchange.** By Prof. W. Stanley Jevons, F.R.S. Part I.

No. 51. **Money and the Mechanism of Exchange.** Part II.

No. 52. **The Diseases of the Will.** By Th. Ribot. Translated from the French by J. Fitzgerald, M.A.

No. 53. **Animal Automatism,** and other Essays. By Prof. T. H. Huxley, F.R.S.

No. 54. **The Birth and Growth of Myth.** By Edward Clodd, F.R.A.S.

No. 55. **The Scientific Basis of Morals,** and other Essays. By William Kingdon Clifford, F.R.S.

No. 56. **Illusions.** By James Sully. Part. I.

No. 57. **Illusions.** Part II.

No. 58. **The Origin of Species.** By Charles Darwin. Part I. (Double number).

No. 59. **The Origin of Species.** Part II. (Double Number).

No. 60. **The Childhood of the World.** By Edward Clodd, F.R.A.S.

No. 61. **Miscellaneous Essays.** By Richard A. Proctor.

No. 62. **The Religions of the Ancient World.** By Prof. Geo. Rawlinson, Univ. of Oxford. (Double number).

No. 63. **Progressive Morality.** By Thomas Fowler, LL.D, President of Corpus Christi Coll., Oxford.

No. 64. **The Distribution of Animals and Plants.** By A. Russell Wallace and W. T. Thistleton Dyer.

No. 65. **Conditions of Mental Development,** and other Essays. By William Kingdon Clifford.

No. 66. **Technical Education.** and other Essays By Thomas H. Huxley, F.R.S.

No. 67. **The Black Death.** An account of the Great Pestilence of the 14th Century. By J. F. C. Hecker, M.D.

No. 68. **Three Essays.** By Herbert Spencer.

No. 69. **Fetichism:** A Contribution to Anthropology and the History of Religion. By Fritz Schultze, Ph. D. (Double number).

No. 70. **Essays Speculative and Practical.** By Herbert Spencer.

No. 71. **Anthropology.** By Daniel Wilson, Ph. D. With Appendix on Archæology. By E. B. Tylor, F.R.S.

No. 72. **The Dancing Mania of the Middle Ages.** By J. F. C. Hecker, M.D.

No. 73. **Evolution in History, Language and Science.** Four addresses delivered at the London Crystal Palace School of Art, Science and Literature.

No. 74.
No. 75.
No. 76.
No. 77. **The Descent of Man,** and Selection in Relation to Sex. (*Numerous Illustrations*). By Charles Darwin. *Nos.* 74, 75, 76 are *single Nos.; No.* 77 *is a double No.*

No. 78. **Historical Sketch of the Distribution of Land in England.** By William Lloyd Birbeck, M.A.

No. 79. **Scientific Aspect of some Familiar Things.** By W. M. Williams.

No. 80. **Charles Darwin.** His Life and Work. By Grant Allen. (Double Number).

No. 81. **The Mystery of Matter, and the Philosophy of Ignorance.** Two Essays by J. Allanson Picton.

No. 82. **Illusions of the Senses,** and other Essays. By Richard A. Proctor.

No. 83. **Profit-Sharing Between Capital and Labor.** Six Essays. By Sedley Taylor, M.A.

No. 84. **Studies of Animated Nature.** Four Essays on Natural History. By W. S. Dallas, F.L.S., and Others.

No. 85. **The Essential Nature of Religion.** By J. Allanson Picton.

No. 86. **The Unseen Universe,** and the Philosophy of the Pure Sciences. By Prof. Wm. Kingdon Clifford, F.R.S.

No. 87. **The Morphine Habit.** By Dr. B. Ball, of the Paris Faculty of Medicine.

No. 88. **Science and Crime** and other Essays. By Andrew Wilson, F.R.S.E.

No. 89. **The Genesis of Science.** By Herbert Spencer.

No. 90. **Notes on Earthquakes:** with Fourteen Miscellaneous Essays. By Richard A. Proctor.

No 91. **The Rise of Universities.** By S. S. Laurie, LL.D. (Double number).

No. 92. **The Formation of Vegetable Mould through the Action of Earth Worms.** By Charles Darwin, LL.D., F.R.S. (Double number).

No. 93. **Scientific Methods of Capital Punishment.** By J. Mount Bleyer, M D.

No. 94. **The Factors of Organic Evolution.** By Herbert Spencer.

No 95. **The Diseases of Personality.** By Th. Ribot. Translated from the French by J. Fitzgerald, M.A.

No. 96. **A Half-Century of Science.** By Thomas H. Huxley, and Grant Allen.

No. 97. **The Pleasures of Life.** By Sir John Lubbock.

No. 98. **Cosmic Emotion: Also the Teachings of Science.** By William Kingdon Clifford.

No. 99. **Nature Studies.** By Prof. F. R. Eaton Lowe; Dr. Robert Brown, F L S; Geo. G. Chisholm, F.R.G.S.; and James Dallas, F.L.S.

No. 100. **Science and Poetry, with other Essays.** By Andrew Wilson, F.R S.E.

No. 101. **Æsthetics; Dreams and Association of Ideas.** By James Sully and Geo. Croom Robertson.

No. 102. **Ultimate Finance; A True Theory of Co-operation.** By William Nelson Black.

No. 103. **The Coming Slavery: The Sins of Legislators; The Great Political Superstition.** By Herbert Spencer.

No. 104. **Tropical Africa.** By Henry Drummond, F.R.S.

No. 105. **Freedom in Science and Teaching.** By Ernst Haeckel, of the University of Jena. With a prefatory Note by Prof. Huxley.

No. 106. **Force and Energy. A Theory of Dynamics.** By Grant Allen.

No. 107. **Ultimate Finance. A True Theory of Wealth.** By William Nelson Black.

No. 108. **English, Past and Present.** By Richard Chenevix Trench. Part I. (Double number).

No. 109. **English, Past and Present.** Part II.

No. 110. **The Story of Creation. A Plain Account of Evolution.** By Edward Clodd. (Double number).

No. 111. **The Pleasures of Life.** Part II. By Sir John Lubbock.

No. 112. **Psychology of Attention.** By Th. Ribot. Translated from the French by J. Fitzgerald, M.A.

No. 113. **Hypnotism.** Its History and Development. By Fredrik Björnström, M.D., Head Physician of the Stockholm Hospital, Professor of Psychiatry. Late Royal Swedish Medical Councillor. Authorized Translation from the Second Swedish Edition by Baron Nils Posse, M.G., Director of the Boston School of Gymnastics. (Double number).

No. 114. **Christianity and Agnosticism. A Controversy.** Consisting of papers contributed to *The Nineteenth Century* by Henry Wace, D.D., Prof. Thos. H. Huxley, The Bishop of Petersborough, W. H. Mallock, Mrs. Humphrey Ward. (Double number).

No. 115. **Darwinism:** An Exposition of the Theory of Natural Selection, with some of its Applications. By Alfred Russel Wallace, LL.D., F.L.S., etc. Illustrated. Part I. (Double number).

No. 116. **Darwinism.** Illustrated. Part II. (Double number).

No. 117. **Modern Science and Modern Thought.** By S. Laing. Illustrated. (Double number).

No. 118. **Modern Science and Modern Thought.** Part II.

No. 119. **The Electric Light** and The Storing of Electrical Energy. Illustrated. Gerald Molloy, D.D., D.Sc.

No. 120. **The Modern Theory of Heat** and The Sun as a Storehouse of Energy. Illustrated. Gerald Molloy, D.D., D.Sc.

No. 121. **Utilitarianism.** By John Stuart Mill.

No. 122. **Upon the Origin of Alpine and Italian Lakes** and upon Glacial Erosion. Maps and Illustrations. By Ramsey, Ball, Murchison, Studer, Favre, Whymper and Spencer. Part I. (Double number).

No. 123. **Upon the Origin of Alpine and Italian Lakes,** Etc., Etc. Part II.

No. 124. **The Quintessence of Socialism.** By Prof. A. Schäffle.

No. 125. **Darwinism and Politics.** By David G. Ritchie, M.A. **Administrative Nihilism.** By Thomas Huxley, F.R.S.

No. 126. **Physiognomy and Expression.** By P Mantegazza. Illustrated. Part I. (Double number).

No. 127. **Physiognomy and Expression.** Part II. (Double number).

No. 128. **The Industrial Revolution.** By Arnold Toynbee, Tutor of Baliol College, Oxford With a short memoir by B. Jowett. Part I. (Double number).

No. 129. **The Industrial Revolution.** Part II. (Double number).

No. 130. **The Origin of the Aryans.** By Dr. Isaac Taylor. Illustrated. Part I. (Double number).

No. 131. **The Origin of the Aryans.** Part II. (Double number).

No. 132. **The Evolution of Sex.** By Prof. P. Geddes and J. Arthur Thomson. Illustrated. Part I (Double number).

No. 133. **The Evolution of Sex.** Part II. (Double number).

No. 134. **The Law of Private Right.** By George H. Smith. (Double number).

No. 135. **Capital.** A Critical Analysis of Capitalist Production. By Karl Marx. Part I (Double number)

No. 136. **Capital.** Part II (Double number).

No. 137. **Capital.** Part III. (Double number)

No. 138. **Capital.** Part IV. (Double number).

No. 139. **Lightning.** Thunder and Lightning Conductors. Illustrated. By Gerald Molloy, D.D., D.Sc.

No. 140. **What is Music?** With an appendix on How the Geometrical Lines have their Counterparts in Music. By Isaac L. Rice.

No. 141. **Are the Effects of Use and Disuse Inherited?** By William Platt Ball.

No. 142 **A Vindication of the Rights of Woman.** By Mary Wollstonecraft. With an Introduction by Mrs Henry Fawcet. Part I. (Double number).

No. 143. **A Vindication of the Rights of Woman.** Part II. (Double number).

No. 144. **Civilization; Its Cause and Cure.** By Edward Carpenter

No. 145. **Body and Mind.** By William Kingdon Clifford.

No. 146. **Social Diseases and Worse Remedies.** By Thomas H. Huxley, F.R.S.

No. 147. **The Soul of Man under Socialism.** By Oscar Wilde.

No. 148. **Electricity, the Science of the Nineteenth Century.** By E. C. Caillard (Illustrated.) Part I. (Double number).

No. 149. **Electricity.** Part II.

No. 150. **Degeneration; A Chapter in Darwinism.** Illustrated. By E. Ray Lankester, M.A., LL.D., F.R.S.

No. 151. No. 152. **Mental Suggestion.** By Dr. J. Ochorowicz. Part I. (Double number).

No. 153. No. 154. **Mental Suggestion.** Part II. (Double number.)

No. 155. No. 156. **Mental Suggestion.** Part III. (Double number.)

No. 157. No. 158. **Mental Suggestion.** Part IV. (Double number).

No. 159. **Modern Science; The Science of the Future.** By Edward Carpenter.

No. 160. **Studies in Pessimism.** By Schopenhauer.

No. 161. No. 162. **Flowers, Fruits and Leaves.** Illustrated. By Sir John Lubbock, F.R.S. (Double number).

No. 163. No. 164. **Glimpses of Nature.** Illustrated. By Dr. Andrew Wilson, F.R.S.E. Part I. (Double number).

No. 165. **Glimpses of Nature.** Part II.

No. 166. **Problems of the Future.** By Samuel Laing. Part I.

No. 167. **Problems of the Future.** Part II. (Double number).

No. 168. **Problems of the Future.** Part III. (Double number).

No. 169. **The Moral Teachings of Science.** By Arabella B. Buckley.

No. 170. **The Wisdom of Life.** By Schopenhauer. (Double number).

No. 171. **The Mystery of Pain.** By James Hinton.

No. 172. No. 173. No. 174. No. 175. **What is Property?** An inquiry into the Principle of Right and of Government. By P. J. Proudhon. (Four double numbers, $1.20).

No. 176. **The History and Scope of Zoology.** By E. Ray Lankester.

No. 177. **Evolution and Ethics.** By Prof. T. H. Huxley.

LIST OF BOUND BOOKS

..IN..

The Humboldt Library Series.

The volumes of this series are printed on a superior quality of paper, and bound in extra cloth. They are from fifty to seventy-five per cent. cheaper than any other edition of the same books.

STANDARD WORKS BY VARIOUS AUTHORS.

A Vindication of the Rights of Woman. With Strictures on Political and Moral Subjects. By Mary Wollstonecraft. New Edition, with an introduction by Mrs. Henry Fawcett. Cloth $1.00

Electricity: the Science of the Nineteenth Century. A Sketch for General Readers. By E. M. Caillard, author of "The Invisible Powers of Nature." With Illustrations. Cloth . . . . 75 cts

Mental Suggestion. By J. Ochorowicz. Sometime Professor Extraordinarius of Psychology and Nature-Philosophy in the University of Lemberg. With a Preface by Chas. Richet. Translated from the French by J. Fitzgerald, M.A. Cloth $2.00

Flowers, Fruits, and Leaves. By Sir John Lubbock, F.R.S., D.C.L., LL.D. With Ninety-five Illustrations. Cloth . . . . 75 cts

Glimpses of Nature. By Andrew Wilson, F.R.S.E., F.L.S. With Thirty-five Illustrations. Cloth . . . . 75 cts

Problems of the Future, and Essays. By Samuel Laing, author of "Modern Science and Modern Thought," etc. Cloth . . . $1.25

The Naturalist on the River Amazon. A Record of Adventures, Habits of Animals, Sketches of Brazilian and Indian Life, and Aspects of Nature under the Equator, during Eleven Years of Travel. By Henry Walter Bates, F.L.S., Assistant Secretary of the Royal Geographical Society of England. New Edition. Large Type. Illustrated. Cloth $1.00

The Religions of the Ancient World: including Egypt, Assyria and Babylonia, Persia, India, Phœnicia, Etruria, Greece, Rome. By George Rawlinson, M.A., Camden Professor of Ancient History, Oxford, and Canon of Canterbury. Author of "The Origin of Nations," "The Five Great Monarchies," Etc. Cloth . . . . 75 cts

The Rise and Early Constitution of Universities, with a Survey of Mediæval Education. By S. S. Laurie, LL.D., Professor of the Institutes and History of Education in the University of Edinburgh. Cloth . . 75 cts

Fetichism. A Contribution to Anthropology and the History of Religion. By Fritz Schultze, Ph.D Translated from the German by J. Fitzgerald, M.A. Cloth . . . . . 75 cts

Money and the Mechanism of Exchange. By W. Stanley Jevons, M.A., F.R.S., Professor of Logic and Political Economy in the Owens College, Manchester, England. Cloth . . . . 75 cts

On the Study of Words. By Richard Chenevix Trench, D.D., Archbishop of Dublin. Cloth . . . . 75 cts

The Dawn of History. An Introduction to Prehistoric Study. Edited by C. F. Keary, M.A., of the British Museum. Cloth . . 75 cts

Geological Sketches at Home and Abroad. By Archibald Geikie, LL.D., F.R.S., Director-General of the Geological Surveys of Great Britain and Ireland. Cloth . . . . 75 cts

Illusions: A Psychological Study. By James Sully, author of "Sensation and Intuition," "Pessimism," etc. Cloth . . . 75 cts

The Pleasures of Life. Part I. and Part II. By Sir John Lubbock, Bart. Two Parts in One. Cloth . . . . 75 cts.

English, Past and Present. Part I. and Part II. By Richard Chenevix Trench, D.D., Archbishop of Dublin. Two Parts in One. Cloth . . . . 75 cts

Hypnotism: Its History and Present Development. By Fredrik Björnström, M.D., Head Physician of the Stockholm Hospital, Professor of Psychiatry, late Royal Swedish Medical Councillor. Cloth . . 75 cts

The Story of Creation. A Plain Account of Evolution. By Edward Clodd, F.R.A.S. With over eighty illustrations . . . . . 75 cts

Christianity and Agnosticism. A controversy, consisting of papers by Henry Wace, D.D., Prebendary of St. Paul's Cathedral; Principal of King's College, London. Professor Thomas H. Huxley.—W. C. Magee, D.D., Bishop of Petersborough.—W. H. Mallock, Mrs. Humphrey Ward. Cloth . . 75 cts

Darwinism: An Exposition of the Theory of Natural Selection, with some of its applications. By Alfred Russel Wallace, LL.D., F.L.S. With portrait of the author, colored map, and numerous illustrations. Cloth $1.25

The ablest living Darwinian writer.—*Cincinnati Commercial Gazette.*

The most important contribution to the study of the origin of species and the evolution of man which has been published since Darwin's death. —*New York Sun.*

There is no better book than this in which to look for an intelligent, complete, and fair presentation of both sides of the discussion on evolution.—*New York Herald.*

Modern Science and Modern Thought. A Clear and Concise View of the Principal Results of Modern Science, and of the Revolution which they have effected in Modern Thought. With a Supplemental Chapter on Gladstone's "Dawn of Creation" and "Proem to Genesis," and on Drummond "Natural Law in the Spiritual World." By S. Laing. Cloth . . . . 75 cts

Upon the Origin of Alpine and Italian Lakes; and Upon Glacial Erosion. By A. C. Ramsay, F.R.S., Etc.; John Ball, M.R.I.A., F.L.S., Etc.; Sir Roderick I. Murchison, F.R.S., D.C.L., Etc.; Prof. B. Studer, of Berne; Prof. A. Favre, of Geneva; and Edward Whymper. With an Introduction, and Notes upon the American Lakes, by Prof. J. W. Spencer, Ph.D., F.G.S., State Geologist of Georgia. Cloth . . . . 75 cts

Physiognomy and Expression. By Paolo Mantegazza, Senator; Director of the National Museum of Anthropology, Florence; President of the Italian Society of Anthropology. With Illustrations. Cloth $1.00

The Industrial Revolution of the Eighteenth Century in England. Popular Addresses, Notes, and other Fragments. By the late Arnold Toynbee. Tutor of Balliol College, Oxford. Together with a short memoir by B. Jowett, Master of Balliol College, Oxford. Cloth $1.00

The Origin of the Aryans. An Account of the Prehistoric Ethnology and Civilization of Europe. By Isaac Taylor, M.A., Litt. D., Hon. LL.D. Illustrated. Cloth $1.00

The Law of Private Right. By George H. Smith, author of "Elements of Right, and of the Law," and of Essays on "The Certainty of the Law, and the Uncertainty of Judicial Decisions," "The True Method of Legal Education," Etc., Etc. Cloth . . 75 cts

The Evolution of Sex. By Prof. Patrick Geddes and J. Arthur Thomson. With 104 Illustrations. Cloth $1.00

Such a work as this, written by Prof. Geddes who has contributed many articles on the same and kindred subjects to the Encyclopædia Brittannica, and by Mr. J. Arthur Thomson, is not for the specialist, though the specialist may find it good reading, nor for the reader of light literature, though the latter would do well to grapple with it. Those who have followed Darwin, Wallace, Huxley and Haeckel in their various publications, and have heard of the later arguments against heredity brought forward by Prof. Weissman, will not be likely to put it down unread. . . . The authors have some extremely interesting ideas to state, particularly with regard to the great questions of sex and environment in their relation to the growth of life on earth. . . . They are to be congratulated on the scholarly and clear way in which they have handled a difficult and delicate subject.—*Times.*

Capital: A Critical Analysis of Capitalistic Production. By Karl Marx. Translated from the third German edition by Samuel Moore and Edward Aveling, and edited by Frederick Engels. *The only American Edition. Carefully Revised.* Cloth, $1.75

The great merit of Marx, therefore, lies in the work he has done as a scientific inquirer into the economic movement of modern times, as the philosophic historian of the capitalistic era.—*Encyclopædia Brittannica.*

So great a position has not been won by any work on Economic Science since the appearance of *The Wealth of Nations.* . . . All these circumstances invest, therefore, the teachings of this particularly acute thinker with an interest such as cannot be claimed by any other thinker of the present day.—*The Athenæum.*

What is Property? An Inquiry into the Principle of Right and of Government. By P. J. Proudhon. Cloth $2.00

Thd Philosophy of Misery. A System of Economical Contradictions. By P. J. Proudhon. Cloth $2.00

Works by Professor Huxley.

Evidence as to Man's Place in Nature. With numerous illustrations

AND

On the Origin of Species; or, the Causes of the Phenomena of Organic Nature.

Two books in one volume. Cloth . . . 75 cts

The Physical Basis of Life. With other Essays

AND

Lectures on Evolution. With an Appendix on the Study of Biology.

Two books in one volume. Cloth . . . 75 cts

Animal Automatism

AND

Technical Education, with other Essays.
Two books in one volume. Cloth . . . 75 cts

Select Works of Prof. John Tyndall.

Forms of Water in Clouds and Rivers, Ice and Glaciers. Nineteen illustrations.

Lessons in Electricity. Sixty illustrations.

Six Lectures on Light. Illustrated.
Three books in one volume. Cloth . . . $1.00

Works by Herbert Spencer.

The Data of Ethics. Cloth . . . . . 75 cts

Education: Intellectual, Moral, and Physical,

AND

Progress: Its Law and Cause. With other Disquisitions.
Two books in one volume. Cloth . . . 75 cts

The Genesis of Science,

AND

The Factors of Organic Evolution.
Two books in one volume. Cloth . . . 75 cts

Select Works of Grant Allen.

The Evolutionist at Large.

Vignettes from Nature.

Force and Energy. A Theory of Dynamics.
Three books in one volume. Cloth . . . $1.00

Select Works of Richard A. Proctor, F.R.A.S.

Light Science for Leisure Hours.

Familiar Essays on Scientific Subjects.

Hereditary Traits, and other Essays.

Miscellaneous Essays.

Illusions of the Senses, and other Essays.

Notes on Earthquakes, with Fourteen Miscellaneous Essays.
Six books in one volume $1.50

Select Works of William Kingdon Clifford, F.R.A.S.

Seeing and Thinking.

The Scientific Basis of Morals, and other Essays.

Conditions of Mental Development, and other Essays.

The Unseen Universe.—Also, **The Philosophy of the Pure Sciences.**

Cosmic Emotion.—Also, **The Teachings of Science.**
Five books in one volume. Cloth . . . $1.25

Select Works of Edward Clodd, F.R.A.S.

The Childhood of Religions.

The Birth and Growth of Myths and Legends.

The Childhood of the World.
Three books in one volume. Cloth . . . $1.00

Select Works of Th. Ribot.

The Diseases of Memory.

The Diseases of the Will.

The Diseases of Personality.
Three books in one volume. Cloth . . . $1.00

The Milky Way.

CONTAINING

The Wonders of the Heavens. With thirty-two Actinoglyph Illustrations. By Camille Flammarion.

The Romance of Astronomy. By R. Kalley Miller, M.A.

The Sun: Its Constitution; Its Phenomena; Its Condition. By Nathan T. Carr, LL.D.
Three books in one volume. Cloth . . . $1.00

Political Science.

CONTAINING

Physics and Politics. An Application of the Principles of Natural Selection and Heredity to Political Society. By Walter Bagehot, author of "The English Constitution."

History of the Science of Politics. By Frederick Pollock.
Two books in one volume. Cloth . . . 75 cts

The Land Question.

CONTAINING

The History of Landholding in England. By Joseph Fisher, F.R.H.S.

Historical Sketch of the Distribution of Land in England. By William Lloyd Birkbeck, M.A.
Two books in one volume. Cloth . . . 75 cts

www.ingramcontent.com/pod-product-compliance
Lightning Source LLC
Chambersburg PA
CBHW022155020726
47496CB00008B/2733